Private jets. Luxury cars. Exclusive five-star hotels. Designer outfits for every occasion and an entourage of staff to see to your every whim. In this brand-new collection, ordinary women step into the world of the superrich and are

TAKEN BY THE MILLIONAIRE

Don't miss any of this month's offerings:

HEIDI RICE was born and bred and still lives in London, England. She has two boys who love to bicker, a wonderful husband who, luckily for everyone, has loads of patience, and a supportive and ever-growing British/French/Irish/American family. As much as Heidi adores "the Big Smoke," she also loves America, and every two years or so she and her best friend leave hubby and kids behind and *Thelma and Louise* it across the States for a couple of weeks (although they always leave out the driving-off-a-cliff bit). She's been a film buff since her early teens and a romance junkie for almost as long. She indulged her first love by being a film reviewer for the last ten years. Then, two years ago, she decided to spice up her life by writing romance. Discovering the fantastic sisterhood of romance writers (both published and unpublished) in Britain and America made it a wild and wonderful journey to writing for Harlequin, and she's looking forward to many more books to come.

Heidi loves to hear from her readers. Contact her by visiting her Web site at www.heidi-rice.com or e-mailing her at heidi@heidi-rice.com.

Heidi Rice

The Millionaire's Blackmail Bargain

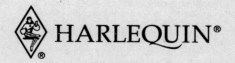

HARLEQUIN®

TORONTO • NEW YORK • LONDON
AMSTERDAM • PARIS • SYDNEY • HAMBURG
STOCKHOLM • ATHENS • TOKYO • MILAN • MADRID
PRAGUE • WARSAW • BUDAPEST • AUCKLAND

ISBN-13: 978-0-373-82095-5
ISBN-10:   0-373-82095-X

THE MILLIONAIRE'S BLACKMAIL BARGAIN

First North American Publication 2008.

Previously published in the UK under the title
THE MILE-HIGH CLUB.

The Millionaire's Blackmail Bargain

For my mum, Sylvia, because she's magnificent.
With special thanks to my sister-in-law Isabel
for making Jack fluent in French (unlike me).

CHAPTER ONE

CARMEL ROURKE strained to hear the footsteps in the bedroom next door, crouched against the cold enamel of the bath and tried not to breathe. Now, if she could just stop her heartbeat sounding like the cannon-fire finale from the 1812 Overture, she might be able to avoid spending Christmas in a prison cell.

How had she ended up hiding in The Ritz hotel bathroom of a complete stranger? And how had her life taken another sharp turn into the toilet without her seeing it coming?

This time, it was all Louisa's stupid fault.

Trust her so-called friend Louisa to come up with a hare-brained scheme that would get Louisa a promotion and probably a Pulitzer Prize, if they pulled it off—and land Mel in jail if they didn't. Never listen to a woman who can eat like a trucker and still fit into a size six. People like that never paid for their crimes. Mel, on the other hand, only had to look at a chocolate bar and it went straight to her hips.

The footsteps from next door stopped. Mel sucked in another breath and held it. She heard the bedsprings give a muffled crunch and then the *Ten O'Clock News* blared out its signature tune. Blast, now she wouldn't be able to hear if the guy was coming in here or not. Time to start praying.

Please don't let him come in here. Please don't let him come in here.

Mel recited the mantra in her head as sweat trickled down between her breasts. Her cotton blouse and wool skirt were suffocating her. Her stomach growled, reminding her she hadn't eaten anything since her lunchtime yoghurt. Fabulous, it would be just her luck to pass out from starvation. Good to know she'd be able to fit into a smaller-sized prison uniform.

She leaned her head back against the tiles, stared at the gleaming silver showerhead above her and tried to piece together how exactly she'd ended up in this predicament in the first place—staring starvation, humiliation and almost certain arrest in the face.

It had all begun at the book launch when Louisa had spotted 'the hunk'.

'I'm telling you, I bet you anything it's him,' Louisa whispered in Mel's ear, downing her third sandwich in a row.

'It's not him, Louisa,' Mel insisted as the bookstore manager at the head of the crowd continued to wax lyrical about the latest soon-to-be best-seller from the mysterious crime novelist known only as Devlin. 'I don't care what you've read in *Vanity Fair*. Devlin doesn't do publicity; he'd be nuts to turn up at his own book launches incognito.'

In the last five years, Devlin had become a worldwide publishing sensation. His sales, though, hadn't outstripped the furious press speculation about his hidden identity. Louisa was one of the many reporters clamouring to unmask him. But in Mel's humble editorial assistant's opinion, the book-launch idea was a wild one, even for Louisa.

They'd been there for nearly twenty minutes listening to the bookstore manager drone on about Devlin's 'punishing prose' and 'atmospheric allegories' while Louisa worked her way through the curly sandwiches on the refreshment table—and not one person had piqued even Louisa's vivid imagination.

Then 'the hunk' walked in.

Mel saw him first, standing alone at the back of the shop. She didn't like tall men, she found them intimidating, but, goodness, this guy was striking. Tall, dark and handsome didn't even begin to cover it.

The thick, wavy black hair that curled round his ears, his tanned face, dark slashing brows and a physique that Mel guessed he must spend hours in the gym every day to maintain gave him the look of a modern-day pirate. New blue jeans, black leather boots and a simple black crew-neck sweater only enhanced the romantic image. Mel wondered what colour his eyes might be, when he turned and his gaze locked on hers. A deep, almost translucent blue, it turned out. His eyes flicked down her frame in a way she should have found insulting but her pulse-rate was too busy speeding up to hyperdrive. He seemed to be focused on her forever, although it could only have been a few seconds.

When he turned his attention back to the bookstore manager, Mel's breath gushed out. She tore her eyes away from him, annoyed with herself. He looked like all God-blessed people. Confident. Arrogant. Overwhelming. The sort of guy who turned heads and knew it. The sort of guy she'd sworn off for life.

Mel hadn't pointed 'the hunk' out to Louisa. She knew exactly where her friend's imagination would run with it. She hadn't been wrong.

'Who is he and what's he doing here, then?' Louisa continued. 'He's not a reporter, I'd know him if he was. And he's not talking to the publishing people either.'

'He's probably some guy who's wandered in off the street to see what's going on.'

'He's leaving.' Louisa dumped her sandwich plate on a pile of books and grabbed Mel's arm. 'Let's follow him.'

Before she could blink, Mel was being hauled down Piccadilly, dodging pedestrians as Louisa tried to keep up with the mysterious stranger's long strides. Five minutes later they were both standing breathless outside the entrance to The Ritz.

'You see, I told you,' Mel said between pants. 'He's a tourist. Thank goodness he didn't spot us stalking him down the street.'

'Wait here. I've got an idea.'

Mel frowned as Louisa dashed into the hotel. It was cold, it was starting to rain, she'd left her coat at the bookstore, she was hungry and she wanted to go home.

Mel was still frowning when Louisa burst back through the doors five freezing minutes later, her eyes lit up like the Christmas decorations flanking the hotel's entrance.

'Mel, it's definitely, definitely him.' Louisa clasped her hands together in mock prayer, gazed up at the ornate stone pillars of The Ritz entrance plaza. 'Thank you, God.' She smiled at Mel. 'That silly old bag Dansworth cannot pass me over for promotion again when I land this story on her desk.'

Mel knew she shouldn't encourage it, but even her curiosity was piqued. 'What makes you think the guy's Devlin?'

'Colin works here as the bell manager.'

What? 'Who's Colin?'

'Colin, my second-but-last ex. You know, he always used to call you babe and make you grind your teeth.'

'Okay, so what did Colin have to say?' This should be good. Colin was a moron if Mel's memory served her correctly.

'The guy's registered under the name Dempsey. He's staying in the Royal Suite, one of the most expensive suites in the whole hotel. And Colin says one of the bell boys was crowing when the guy arrived a week ago because he had to deliver a pricey new laptop to his suite and got a twenty-pound tip for his trouble.'

'Okay.' Mel considered the information. 'So he's a rich, computer nerd tourist. So what?'

Louisa grinned, the light in her eyes undimmed. 'Mel.' Her fingers dug into Mel's arm. 'Colin has a passkey.'

'So?'

'Don't be dense. The guy's gone into the restaurant to have dinner. Colin will let you into his suite. All you have to do is find out if he's really who he says he is.'

'What? Are you completely insane?' Mel resisted the urge to shout, but only just. 'That's completely illegal. And why should I do it? I'm a lowly editorial assistant. You're the reporter.'

'You write the book-review column,' Louisa said, missing the point entirely.

'Only because Dansworth doesn't think anyone bothers to read it,' Mel replied, grudgingly. She'd worked long and hard to get the opportunity to write the book reviews; it was the only thing she really enjoyed about her job at *London Nights*.

'It'll only take you a few minutes,' Louisa pleaded.

Mel shivered, suddenly feeling very uneasy. 'I still don't see why you can't do it?'

Louisa looked more sheepish than Bo Peep. 'I'm sort of going to be busy with Colin. He's not risking arrest for nothing, you know.'

Mel's jaw dropped. 'You're not seriously going to prostitute yourself for the sake of a story which probably isn't even a story?'

Louisa waved her hand impatiently. 'Colin happens to be a great kisser.' She reached into her bag and pulled out her press card. 'If anyone catches you…' she paused dramatically '…which they won't—you can say you're me.' She thrust the card into Mel's hand. 'The picture's so faded now, no one will be able to tell you're not me. I'll take any flak, I promise.' Louisa pushed her glossy mane of blonde hair back from her face. 'Mel, you know the magazine needs a boost. We've been dropping circulation for months now. There have even been rumours we might fold.'

'I hadn't heard that.' Mel thought, shocked. She needed this job. The mortgage on her tiny, shoebox-sized flat in West London was enormous and it wasn't going to pay itself.

'Mel.' Louisa's tone became sombre, her eyes serious. 'If I'm prepared to make this sacrifice with Colin to save our colleagues from redundancy, you ought to be prepared to make one too.'

Mel listened to her stomach rumble above the blare of the telly next door.

How come Louisa's sacrifice involved being taken to paradise by Colin the 'great kisser' while hers involved crouching in a hotel bathtub half the night waiting to be carted off to jail?

Her life had become a complete mess. She gave a heavy sigh. And most of it was her own fault, not Louisa's.

Sure, Louisa had led her into this stupid situation, but why had she let herself be led? She should have told Louisa she wouldn't do it. That she couldn't spy on some guy she didn't even know. But she hadn't thought to say it until she was alone in his hotel suite, looking at a worn leather jacket draped over one of the sofas. Just as she'd realised there was no way she could snoop through the guy's stuff, she'd heard the click of his keycard in the door lock.

Mel rolled her shoulders, the cramped conditions in the bathtub making her ache in some very inventive places. She clutched her bag tighter, her palms damp.

How many more stupid mistakes was she going to make in her life?

The thought had a picture of Adam popping into her head.

Handsome, arrogant, deceitful Adam. His charming smile, his carefully toned body, the constant reminders that she ought to watch her own weight. Adam, who she'd thought was her friend—but who was really her biggest mistake to date. What a complete fool she'd been not to see what he was.

The pristine tones of the newsreader shut off. Mel swallowed. Oh, no. She'd been so busy thinking about Adam the Rat, she still hadn't come up with a decent plan.

Jack Devlin threw the TV remote onto the bed and paced over to the window. Drawing the thick velvet drapes, he looked down at night-time Piccadilly, two floors below. The festive lights hooked to the streetlights sparkled on the slick pavement. The rain had stopped, but the Christmas shoppers and night owls huddled at the bus stop across the street still looked cold and miserable.

Dragging a hand through his hair, Jack scowled. He knew just how they felt.

What the hell was the matter with him? It had been three months now and he still couldn't shake it. The boredom. The restlessness. The emptiness inside him.

He let the curtain fall back into place and walked over to the room's well-stocked mini-bar. He spotted the laptop he'd bought a week ago, still in its case. Ignoring it, he grabbed one of the fancy little bottles and splashed the pricey Scottish malt into a glass.

Of course, the whole 'mystery man' fiasco wasn't helping much. He was tired of living in hotel rooms, skulking about to keep ahead of the damn reporters. He didn't want to give the press conference his publishers and his agent were insisting on, but what choice did he have? He was sick of being hunted.

He gulped the liquor down in one shot, grimaced when it burned the back of his throat.

How ironic. When he'd been a kid, he'd always figured money and success would solve all his problems. Right at this moment, two of his books were in *The New York Times* best-seller list and his broker practically had an orgasm every time he spoke to the guy about his investments.

He owned property in Paris, New York and Bermuda. And

yet he couldn't settle anywhere. He felt as if he were reaching for something that wasn't there.

Jack slapped the glass down on the mini-bar. Get over yourself, Devlin.

The empty feeling would pass, eventually. It always had before.

He needed to stop brooding. Getting out of the hotel would be a start. He could check out one of the local bars; what he needed was a change of scene. Staring at the hotel's silk-papered walls for the rest of the evening was not an option—he'd been doing that for most of the past week and it hadn't helped a bit.

The stroll down the road to the bookshop earlier had been a start, he thought wryly. At least it had got his mind off his lack of inspiration for a little while.

He recalled the girl he'd spotted at the launch. She'd certainly been an intriguing diversion. She hadn't been conventionally beautiful, not like the blonde Amazon standing next to her, but there was something about her. He hadn't been able to stop looking at her. Her eyes had fixed on him too. They'd been a soft mossy green, he remembered clearly, bright and intelligent. The directness of her gaze had bothered him a little, but he'd still got a good look at her figure. The boxy blouse she'd worn hadn't really suited her, but he could tell she had some nice curves underneath. He'd broken eye contact first. The reckless urge to make a move on her surprising him. Hell, he'd been in a room full of reporters.

Jack rubbed his chin, felt the day-old stubble. He needed a shave and a shower. Maybe he'd get real lucky and the intriguing girl and her friend would be having a late-night drink in one of the bars around here. He started to whistle as he pulled his sweater and T-shirt over his head, threw them on the bed and pushed open the bathroom door.

* * *

Mel fisted her hands to stop them trembling and sank down further into the bath as the light flashed on. A dark shape crossed in front of the gauzy layers of the shower curtain.

He looked enormous.

But at least he was whistling. Maybe he wouldn't mind when he found a mad woman hiding in his bathroom? She swallowed and prayed her stomach wouldn't grumble. The fear and the hours she'd spent in confinement were making her head start to spin. Then the whistling stopped. Was that the hum of an electric shaver?

Mel tried to inch upright without putting her head too far over the lip of the bath. She needed to be ready to put her plan—pathetic as it was—into action. The electric hum stopped and the whistling started again. Then came the deafening crackle of a zipper and the thud of something hitting the floor. Mel felt her heart jump into her throat and had to suppress the yelp when a tanned, muscled forearm sprinkled with dark hair appeared above her and grasped the shower control.

Two quick twists and a deluge of cold water shot out of the showerhead. Mel squealed as the icy spray hit her full in the face.

'What the…?'

The shower curtain whipped back and towering over her was the hunk—without a stitch on. A sprinkling of dark hair defined the contours of a hard-muscled chest and arrowed down to his groin. Mel's blood pressure shot up to boiling point as her eyes followed the arrow down completely of their own accord. Through the deluge of warming water, she saw something she knew she'd never forget as long as she lived. Her gaze rocketed back up to his face so fast it was a wonder she didn't get whiplash. Piercing blue eyes glared at her, accusingly. But he made no move to cover himself.

Mel pushed the dripping hair off her forehead, her hand shaking so hard she thought she might be having a stroke.

'What the hell are you doing in my bathroom?'

Mel tried to scramble up. She dropped her bag, slipping back as the shower spray continued to pummel her. 'Could you turn it off?' Her voice came out on a pathetic whimper.

He waited several beats, before reaching out and turning off the spray, his eyes glaring at her the whole time.

She stood up, slowly, keeping her eyes trained on his face as if her life depended on it. She would not look down. She would not. Her skin must be vermillion by now and she couldn't control the tremors raking her body. At last, he let go of the curtain, reached behind him and took one of the small towels from the rack. The quick glimpse of a tight male butt made Mel gasp.

He turned back sharply, wrapping the towel firmly around his waist and tucking it in.

Still, he didn't say anything, just pinned her with that forbidding look in his vivid blue eyes. Even with the added height of the bath beneath her, Mel realised he was still taller than her. He had to be at least six feet two or three.

His gaze dipped to her chest.

Mel glanced down at herself and gaped in horror. The water had made her blouse and bra transparent. Her puckered nipples were clearly visible through the sodden material. She clasped her arms across her chest, clung onto her shoulders, but couldn't control the trembling or the hot flush racing up her neck. Could this actually get any worse?

'You better get out,' he said, his voice ominously calm.

He stepped back, letting her climb out, and then turned to reach for another of the towels on the shelf opposite.

A flash of adrenaline surged through Mel. Stop being a ninny and get out of here.

She launched herself across the bathroom, her feet sliding on the wet tiles as she clutched the door handle and lurched into the bedroom.

She heard the pad of footsteps behind her and tried to speed up.

'Oh, no, you don't, honey.'

The words seemed to boom in her ear as strong arms wrapped around her from behind and hauled her back against a solid male chest. Her feet lifted off the floor. Frantic, she shoved her elbow back, heard a muffled grunt. But his grip on her only tightened, pressing her heaving breasts against warm, hard forearms. The spicy scent of his aftershave filled her nostrils.

'Stop struggling. I'm not going to hurt you. I want to know who you are and what the hell you're doing here.'

The buzzing in Mel's ears became deafening. Don't you dare faint, you idiot. As she registered the thought her skin flashed hot and then everything went black.

CHAPTER TWO

MEL snuggled into the cosy warmth, her nose wrinkling at the delicious scent of home-cooked meat. Mum must have done dinner. Thank goodness—she was ravenous. She gave a lazy sigh and opened her eyes.

And shot straight up in bed.

This was not her childhood bedroom. The last dregs of the comforting dream swept away as she became aware of exactly where she was and with whom. A bedside lamp illuminated 'the hunk' who sat in an armchair a few feet away, watching her. A slow smile spread across his face.

'Hello, sleeping beauty.' The rough intimacy of the words made the flush creep into Mel's cheeks.

Well, at least he'd put his clothes back on. The thought had her looking down at herself in trepidation. She breathed a sigh of relief and gripped the lapels of the hotel's fluffy monogrammed bathrobe. She pulled them together to hide the glimpse of white cotton underwear beneath. She didn't know how she'd got undressed and she didn't want to know.

'How you feeling?' he said.

Mel's fingers fisted on the robe. 'I'm fine, thank you.'

She needed to make a move and quickly, before he asked any more questions. Lifting the bed's thick, satin duvet, Mel swung her feet to the floor.

'I should be going,' she said briskly, trying to keep the cumbersome robe wrapped around her bare legs. 'I'm really sorry to intrude on you like this. Basically, I got the wrong room and when I heard you come in I panicked.'

The pathetic excuse was the best she'd come up with after hours of squatting in the bathtub.

The quizzical raising of one dark brow made it clear her host wasn't too impressed with it either. Without saying anything, he picked up what looked like a credit card and tapped it absently on the table beside him.

'You're gonna have to do better than that.' He glanced at the card. 'Ms Louisa DiMarco of *London Nights* magazine.'

Mel's eyes widened. He had Louisa's press card. 'You went through my bag!'

He smiled, but his eyes sharpened as he leaned forward, propping his elbows on his knees. 'Damn straight I did, Louisa. When I find a strange woman invading my privacy, I figure the least I should do is return the favour.'

'Yes, well,' Mel mumbled and stared down at her toes. Guilt washed over her. He had a point. She tugged on her lip, looked up. 'I'm sorry about that. Maybe if I get out of your way now we could forget about the whole thing.'

She hopped off the bed, still clutching the robe. The tension in her shoulders eased a bit when he leaned back in his chair. He looked relaxed and amused.

'Um.' She glanced round the elegantly furnished bedroom. 'Where are my clothes?'

'Well, now.' He smiled again. 'You got a problem there, Louisa. The bell hop has them.'

'What? Why?'

'They were soaking wet.' He stood up. 'I told him to send them off to the cleaners and have them back by morning.'

She should have thanked him for his thoughtfulness, but

she had the distinct feeling he hadn't sent her clothes off to be considerate.

'Now, you could leave without them,' he continued in the same smug tone of voice, dropping Louisa's press card on the table.

He stepped towards her. She sat back on the bed.

'But then I'd have to insist on having this back.' He tugged on the sleeve of her robe. It fell off her shoulder. She scrambled to pull it back up. 'Which would leave you wandering around the hotel in nothing but that cute little bra and panties. This being The Ritz, I'll bet the management's got rules about that sort of thing.'

Mel's cheeks ignited. If he'd wanted to get his own back on her for 'invading his privacy', he'd certainly done it in spades.

Just when she was sure her humiliation couldn't be any more complete, her stomach growled. Oh, please, give me a break.

He laughed. The rough sound sent a strange quiver up her spine.

'I ordered up a couple of steaks. They're in the other room if you want to join me for supper.'

Actually, she wanted to tell him to take his steak and shove it up his nose. If he'd stayed and had dinner in the restaurant earlier as he was supposed to, none of this would have happened. But the smell from the room next door was delicious and it didn't look as if she was going to be able to leave any time soon. Her stomach grumbled again. It had to be at least eleven o'clock now, she was starving and she needed to keep her wits about her if she was going to be stuck in his company for the rest of the night.

Mel gave a stiff nod. 'Thanks, that's nice of you.'

She kept her head high, her back straight and the robe wrapped tight as she walked past him. But the plush softness of the towelling against her skin and the silky texture of the carpeting beneath her bare feet made her far too aware of the fact that she was practically naked, in a hotel room with a strange man in the middle of the night.

Louisa would die a slow and painful death as soon as she got out of here.

Jack grinned as his uninvited guest waltzed into the sitting room in front of him—clinging on to her dignity almost as tightly as the oversized bathrobe.

Well, one thing was for sure. He wasn't bored any more and he had his fascinating trespasser to thank for it.

It had been a shock finding her in his bathtub, but he'd got over it quick enough once he'd felt her wet and wriggling in his arms. He was a firm believer in making the best of whatever life threw at you. Life had thrown plenty at Jack Devlin, but never anything quite this cute and appealing.

Even dripping wet, her chestnut hair obscuring those round green eyes and her lush little figure displayed to its full effect in her sodden clothing, Jack had recognised her straight away.

She was the girl from the book launch.

It had given him a hell of a jolt when she'd passed out cold in his arms, but once he was sure she was okay and had drifted into a deep sleep he'd been pretty damn noble. He'd hesitated at first about getting her out of her soaking wet clothes, but when she'd started shivering violently he'd figured he didn't have much of a choice. So he'd peeled her out of them as gently as he could, put on the robe and tucked her into the hotel bed without taking a single liberty. Well, okay, he had got a good look at her—the practical white cotton underwear more sexy somehow than a whole catalogue full of Victoria's Secret—but he hadn't touched, not more than was absolutely necessary. He ought to get a medal for that, especially when she'd sighed in her sleep and he'd caught a whiff of some heady scent that made his blood surge as it hadn't since he was a teenager.

Of course, it wasn't until he'd found out who she was that he'd decided to send her clothes off to the cleaners.

A reporter.

Of all the women to have this reaction to. His radar must have been off earlier, because it hadn't even occurred to him she might be a snoop. But as he'd watched her sleeping, even knowing the miserable, underhanded things she did for a living, the strong feeling of attraction hadn't gone away.

What the heck, Jack had figured after a while. Why not turn the tables on her? Payback had distinct possibilities.

Jack held her chair out for her and waited as she pulled the folds of the robe around her and sat down. The lapels fell forward, giving him another tantalising glimpse of the simple cotton covering her full breasts. This could be fun.

'So, Louisa, why don't you tell me how you really ended up in my bathtub?'

Mel shuffled forward on her seat and anchored the robe beneath her before looking up at him. She ought to tell him who she really was. But seeing that self-assured look in his eyes, she couldn't do it. He looked like a cat who'd just found a nice plump mouse to swallow.

Surely, letting him believe she was Louisa wasn't such a big crime? After all, Louisa should have been here instead of her anyway.

'It's sort of a long story,' she mumbled back, not quite able to push aside the stab of guilt at her dishonesty.

'No problem.' He lifted a covered plate off the hostess trolley and put it in front of her. 'We've got all night, remember?'

Mel studied him as he reached for his own plate. Tall, dark, handsome—and with an ego the size of London. She had the definite impression he was enjoying her discomfort. And what was with all those smouldering looks he kept giving her?

He took the large, domed brass cover off her plate. The smell of the perfectly cooked steak and dauphinoise potatoes made saliva pool in her mouth.

She picked up her napkin just as he plopped the cover back on the plate.

Her eyes jerked to his.

'No supper till you answer my question, Louisa.'

Now that was just plain mean.

Mel dumped her napkin back on the table. Oh, what the hell? She might as well come clean about that at least. She couldn't look much dafter than she did already—and she wanted that steak.

'I thought you were Devlin.'

He cocked an eyebrow. 'Who?'

'Devlin, the mystery novelist.'

He stared at her blankly.

'You know, the number-one best-selling author in most of the known galaxy,' she prompted.

'The writer guy? The one whose book they're selling at the store down the street?'

'Yes.' Okay, maybe she could look dafter. 'That would be Devlin.'

His lips quirked, the spark of amusement in his eyes making them look even more blue. How irritating. 'What gave you that idea?' he said, his tone incredulous.

'Honestly, at this precise moment I haven't got a clue.'

His shoulders jerked and he chuckled. 'Now I get it,' he said. 'You snuck into my hotel suite and hid in my bathtub so you could what? Interview me in my birthday suit?'

Mel's cheeks flushed at the memory of him, naked and furious, standing over her while the shower drenched her.

The chuckles turned to laughs. Mel noticed a slight cleft in his chin, which made his face look even more masculine and appealing.

Okay, so the notion he might be Devlin was a stupid one. Thank you, Louisa. But did he have to find it quite so hilarious?

As he continued to laugh, sitting down in the chair opposite her and wiping his eyes with his napkin, Mel felt a strange sensation in her chest. Maybe it was stress, or fatigue, or just the roller coaster of emotions she'd been on the last few hours, but suddenly a small giggle burst out. She clasped her hand over her mouth, but as his laughter rumbled out, the sound rough and carefree, her shoulders began to relax and before she knew it she was laughing right along with him.

Eventually, the storm of mirth eased down to the odd chuckle, the odd giggle between them.

He barked out one last laugh as he leaned forward and took a wine bucket from the bottom of the hostess trolley. 'I think we both deserve a drink,' he said, lifting out an icy bottle of Chardonnay. 'Grab the glasses, Louisa. They're on the bottom of the trolley.'

She set the crystal wine goblets on the small table, and he poured the light amber liquid into them. He handed her a glass, picked up his own and winked. 'Here's to you, Louisa DiMarco. That's the best entertainment I've had in a long while.'

'Glad to be of service,' she replied, the tinkle of crystal and the gleam of appreciation in his gaze adding to the celebratory mood.

He'd seen the funny side of her stupid stunt and he hadn't called the police. Really, things could have been a whole lot worse now that she thought about it. She took a sip of the cold wine; the tart, fruity taste made her tastebuds moan.

He lifted the cover back off her plate. 'Eat up, Slim. You've earned it.'

He didn't have to ask her twice. She savoured each bite of the delicious meal, letting the tastes explode on her tongue. She'd pay for it tomorrow, when she had to have yoghurt for lunch again, but who cared? She deserved a treat.

He ate with equal enthusiasm, pausing only to refill their glasses as he polished off the meal. Finishing ahead of her, he took his wineglass in his hand and pushed his chair back, crossing his long legs in front of him.

'So, Louisa, how long have you been an investigative reporter?'

She could tell from the spark of amusement in his eyes and the light tone of his voice that he was teasing her, but, frankly, she didn't care. Her stomach was pleasantly full, the robe felt warm and soft and the two glasses of wine had made her feel very mellow indeed.

This wasn't real life. This was a delicious candlelit dinner with a devastatingly attractive man in The Ritz Hotel. She was Mata Hari and Kate Moss all rolled into one. She could play whatever part she wanted tonight and no one would be any the wiser.

'Not long enough, obviously,' she said. The tanned skin around his eyes creased as he smiled at the tart remark. The warm, liquid spot low in her belly got bigger.

As she watched him pour them both another glass of wine it dawned on Mel she hadn't found out a thing about him. He had a slight American accent, which lacked the harsh twang of most tourists, but that didn't tell her much. She didn't even know his name. Time to put Mata Hari to work.

'So what do you do—when you're not writing best-selling novels, that is?'

He hesitated for a second, returning the wine bottle to its bucket with a plop. 'Shoes,' he said, eventually. 'Um, I work in shoes.'

'Shoes?' How peculiar. 'Are you a designer?'

'No.' He looked affronted. 'I sell them.'

'You're a shoe salesman!' Mel giggled. She couldn't help it. He had to be the most unlikely shoe salesman she'd ever seen in her life. 'But how comes you're staying at The Ritz?'

'I happen to be a very good shoe salesman.'

She lifted her glass. 'Here's to—' She paused, lowered her glass. 'Sorry, I don't know your name.'

'The name's Jack. Jack Dempsey.'

Mel tapped her glass to his. 'Here's to Jack Dempsey. Who's a much better shoe salesman than I am an investigative reporter.' Wasn't that the truth?

Then she hiccupped.

'Uh-oh,' Jack said, easing the glass out of her hand. 'I think someone's had enough wine for one night.'

As much as Jack was enjoying the flushed look on her face and the definite spark of flirtation in the air, he had no intention of letting his pretty little guest get hammered. Warm and willing and responsive was what he wanted tonight, and, from the way things were going, he figured he had a good chance of getting it.

'You better stick to water for the time being, Slim,' he said as he poured her a glass from the jug on the table. 'Here you go.'

'Thanks.' She reached out to take it and the robe slipped off her shoulder for about the hundredth time that evening. She pulled it up absently, obviously unaware of the effect it was having on his libido.

For a reporter, she seemed artless and even a little unsure of herself. Jack figured it had to be an illusion, but, even so, it was killing him.

She took a long gulp of the water, looking at him over the rim of the glass. 'Why do you keep calling me Slim?' she asked. 'Are you teasing me?'

'No.' He considered the question for a moment. 'It's weird, but Louisa doesn't fit somehow.' She shifted her eyes back to her plate, her cheeks reddening. Damn, but it was irresistible the way she blushed all the time. 'Anyhow,' he continued, wondering if he could get her to blush some more, 'you know what they say. If the name fits…'

'You are teasing me.' Her face fell.

What had he said wrong? 'No, I'm not.'

'You and I both know I'm not slim. So don't call me that.'

Jack put his glass down. Was she for real? Surely no one could be that clueless about how pretty they were. 'Is this one of those "does my bum look big in this?" moments you English girls are so keen on? Cos if it is, I'm telling you straight, I'm not having that conversation. I already know it's a no-win situation for me.'

Mel blinked and stared at the man in front of her. Was he flirting with her? The dark appreciation was obvious in his eyes as they swept her face. Yes, he was. The sudden realisation had a strange effect on the place between her legs. She squeezed her thighs together.

It had been such a long time since anyone had flirted with her, she'd forgotten how good it felt. A giddy little rush of anticipation and excitement swept through her.

Don't get carried away. She forced herself to calm down. You still don't know a thing about him. 'Are you from America?' she asked.

His brow creased. 'Yeah. Idaho.'

'Will you be here long?'

He seemed to think about the question for a while. 'My flight home's tomorrow afternoon.'

Mel's pulse throbbed.

Why shouldn't they go for it? No guilt, no commitments, no analysing everything to death. She'd always gone for the safe option. Jack Dempsey was the complete opposite of the safe option. Wildly attractive, devilishly sexy, clearly a confident womaniser. Why not let him lead the way? She was twenty-seven years old—and she'd never been seduced in her life. And certainly not by a man who looked like he did.

As if on cue, he leaned forward, took hold of her hand.

Turning it over, he drew his thumb across her palm. The blue of his eyes seemed to deepen, intensify. Talk about smouldering looks. 'You know, we've got the rest of the night to get through. Seems kind of a shame not to make the most of it,' he said, softly.

Mel swallowed. Could she go through with this? 'How do you mean?'

'Don't look so scared; we're not going to do anything you don't want to do. It's only…' he paused, cocked his head to one side '…I've been wanting to kiss you ever since I spotted you tonight at the book launch.'

'You have?' Oh, be quiet, woman, you sound like a twit.

He grinned, apparently not appalled by her complete lack of sophistication. 'Yeah, I have.' With her hand still in his, he stood up. 'You want to give it a shot?' Dropping his napkin on the table, he pulled her upright.

Give it a shot? Mel thought. Oh, yes, please.

He rested his palm on the small of her back. She could feel the warm pressure through the heavy towelling, tried to relax her breathing as he steered her to the large leather sofa in the middle of the room.

With the lights dimmed and only the sound of their breathing to break the silence, Mel felt cocooned in a luxurious fantasy world.

He sat down and the leather creaked beneath him. Holding her hand, he tugged her neatly into his lap.

'Oh!' She let go of the robe to grip his shoulders. He gave her a slow, lazy smile and she shivered.

'You cold?' he asked as his hands settled on her waist, holding her in place.

'No.' Couldn't he see she was practically on fire?

She studied his wonderfully masculine face in the half-light. The light shadow of stubble was beginning to show on his chin, even though he'd shaved earlier that evening. She breathed in the scent of his soap and aftershave. Her fingers flexed on the firm musculature of his shoulders beneath his T-shirt.

He kept his eyes open and fixed on her as he moved forward. 'Why don't we see if we can warm you up a little more?' he said, his voice low and amused, his lips so close to hers she could feel the light brush of his breath against her cheek.

'All right,' she whispered, not wanting to break the spell.

His hands stroked up her back and her breath clogged in her throat. Her heart was beating painfully in her chest. Threading his fingers through her hair, he lifted it away from her face, then angled her head and placed his lips on hers.

At first the kiss was light, teasing, tempting her to open her mouth. She sighed and let his tongue in. He explored in strong, confident strokes, going deeper, taking more. She moaned as her tongue tangled with his. Her fingers curled hard into his shoulders. The ball of heat blazed up from her core, spreading up her chest and pebbling her nipples.

He stopped, abruptly, holding her head as he pulled back. His ragged breathing matched her own. 'Wow, Louisa, you're really good at that,' he said.

'So are you,' she replied.

Jack could see the dark shadow of arousal in her eyes, the redness of her pale skin where he'd devoured her mouth. He hadn't felt that kick of pure, unadulterated lust since he was in high school. He was hard as a brick in his jeans. He shifted, trying to ease the ache. Hell, he wanted to bury himself inside her right now. This wasn't the first time he'd had anonymous sex in his life, but it had never been this intense, this spontaneous before.

He smoothed the hair back from her face with unsteady fingers. The robe had fallen open, revealing the swell of her breasts against the white cotton of her bra. He clamped down on the urge to rip the fabric away and gorge himself on her.

He looked back into her face. Panic as well as passion swirled in her eyes. Calm down, Jack. Don't frighten her. 'I want to look at you, to touch you. Are you okay with that?' They'd moved so fast already he had to be sure.

She nodded. He sent up a small prayer of thanks. Slowly and as carefully as he could, he pushed the robe off her shoulders with shaking hands and let it pool at her waist.

Mel watched as if in a strange erotic dream as his long, tanned fingers eased the cotton covering off her breast. He cupped the weight of her in his palm, skimmed his thumb across the rigid peak. Mel shuddered, gripping his shoulders. Then he bent forward and laved the turgid nipple with his tongue. Heat flooded between her thighs and she moaned. She held his head as he suckled strongly. Darts of fire shot down to her sex, making her melt.

He lifted his head. His hand fumbled for a minute behind her back and the bra loosened. He tugged it off, leaving her naked to the waist. He was still fully dressed, she realised, and drew back slightly.

'Don't panic,' he said gently, as if he had sensed her unease. His hands held her waist. 'I meant what I said—we don't do anything you don't want to.'

'I want to see you too.'

'Okay.' He smiled, the heat in his eyes matching the burning at her centre. 'Come on.' Sliding her off his lap, he stood up. The robe pooled at her feet and he lifted her into his arms. She held onto his neck, amazed he had the strength to pick her up so easily.

The tensed muscles of his forearms were rigid against her naked back and thighs as he carried her into the bedroom. He let her down slowly. The peaks of her nipples rubbed against the worn cotton of his T-shirt. His hands stroked her sides, came to rest on her bottom. He pulled her against him. She felt it then. The hard, shocking evidence of his arousal pushing against the rough denim of his jeans. She looked down, gasped. His muscles weren't the only thing about him that were well developed.

The rough laugh he gave made her eyes dart back up. 'Don't worry, it'll be fine.' His fingers dipped beneath the top of her panties as he said it.

She pulled back. 'Hang on a minute,' she said. 'You're still dressed.' She wanted to touch him so badly now the anticipation was almost more than she could bear.

'Fair point,' he murmured. Taking a small step back, he pulled his T-shirt over his head. His chest looked even more magnificent than she remembered it. Black hair curled across impressive pectoral muscles, thinned across a mouth-watering six-pack and reached down beneath the waistband of his jeans. She stared at the hollows that defined his hipbones. Transfixed, her arms clasped across her chest, she watched as he unbuttoned his fly. The erection sprang forward as he pushed his boxers and his denims off in one movement.

Her mouth dropped open. He looked so much bigger, down there, than he had earlier, and even then he'd looked pretty overwhelming.

He drew her towards him, slipping hot fingers under the waistband of her panties. 'Okay, now it's your turn,' he said, sliding the material down.

Standing naked in front of him, she trembled, sensation pulsing through her body in an intoxicating combination of terror and euphoria.

His hand curled around hers and he led her to the bed. 'Let's get you under the covers—you're shivering.'

She wanted to say she wasn't cold, just the opposite in fact, but as he tucked her beneath the satin duvet, his long, lean body radiating warmth and strength beside her, she couldn't utter a sound.

He cupped her face in his palm, covered her lips with his. As before, the devastating dance of his tongue on hers made her insides dissolve. But now she could feel every inch of him. The hair on his chest, rough against the sensitive peaks of her nipples, the hardness of his thigh as it pressed between her legs and rubbed her centre and the velvet strength of his erection prodding her belly.

His fingers trailed across her inner thigh and probed the slick folds at her core. She moaned, bucked under him, the quick touch electrifying.

'You're so wet.' He groaned, drew his hand away. 'I want to be inside you; are you ready?'

Still she couldn't speak, the rush of passion so intense it robbed her of any coherent thoughts. She nodded and his hands gripped her hips. As he settled between her legs the stiff shaft probed at her entrance.

He stopped, cursed softly and pulled back.

'Wait a minute.' He leaned across her; she could see the grim concentration in his face as he fumbled for a minute in the drawer beside the bed. 'Wouldn't want to forget this,' he said triumphantly, holding the small foil packet and then ripping it open with his teeth. 'Now,' he murmured a few seconds later, holding her hips, angling her body to receive him. 'Where were we?'

He probed for a moment and then thrust within, slowly but surely.

Mel gasped as he lodged inside her. He felt so large, so hard, but beneath the full, stretched feeling the throb of pleasure was so intense she moaned. He dug his fingers into her hips, holding her firm as he began to move, his pelvis brushing the sensitive nub of her sex. In and out, each strong, unstoppable thrust took him deeper inside her. Just when she was sure she couldn't take any more, the crest of pleasure crashed over her, like a tidal wave, making every nerve in her body burst free. She shouted out as the orgasm rolled over her full force, but it didn't stop. It began to build again to another impossible peak as he continued to thrust, harder, faster now.

'Look at me,' he growled against her ear. Her eyes snapped open. She could see the blaze of passion in his face, the desperate intensity in the rigid line of his jaw.

'Do it again for me,' he said, his voice hoarse with need. She couldn't have stopped it now even if she'd wanted to. Her body shook as a pleasure far greater, far more intense than the first time slammed into her. She heard him shout out as she clung onto him and shattered.

CHAPTER THREE

THE insistent patter of rain against glass seeped into Mel's consciousness. She shifted and winced, the muscles in her thighs aching as if she'd just run a marathon. She opened her eyes, flinched and snapped them shut again.

She heard a low grunt, the mattress dipped and the warmth enfolding her slipped away. She squinted, lifting her lids more carefully this time. Thick, dark, wavy hair came into focus, and then wide, naked shoulders cocooned in a pale gold quilt.

Mel inched closer to tug the tiny bit of spare covering back over herself. She stared up at the ceiling, her fingers gripping onto the edge of the quilt, and groaned.

What on earth had she done?

The musty smell of sex hung in the air. But the cold, grey December light coming through the mullioned windows beside the bed had dispelled all the romance from the night before.

Mel held herself rigid under the swatch of duvet.

She'd had a one-night stand with a complete stranger.

And not just any one-night stand. Memories of the night flashed before her, like images from a wildly erotic and particularly graphic X-rated video. He'd done things to her she'd never even dreamt about before.

Even though her brain was tired and fuzzy and her body ached in some very unfamiliar places, she felt the renewal of desire, of arousal. Her nipples pebbled beneath the quilt, as if begging for his tongue. She squeezed her eyes shut and willed the images away. For goodness' sake, one night of unbridled passion and she'd turned into a nymphomaniac.

He shifted again next to her and her eyes jolted open.

He had turned over and his face was next to hers. He looked just as magnificent now in the brittle light of day as he had the night before. Even with his hair crushed down on one side and his beautiful eyes closed, those chiselled cheeks and masculine brows confirmed him as a hunk. Now she knew what he was capable of in bed, she knew how much of a hunk.

But without the cloaking spell of night-time, without the excitement of wine and darkness and anonymity, Mel couldn't figure out how she'd ended up in bed with him. Yes, he was gorgeous, but she didn't know him. She'd been impulsive only once before in her sexual relationships—with Adam the Rat— and even then she hadn't slept with him on their first date.

She studied the face on the pillow next to her again.

Not to put too fine a point on it, she'd been completely and utterly seduced by a shoe salesman from Idaho.

One minute she'd been fluttering her eyelashes at him and the next, he'd been buried deep inside her, sending her into an erotic frenzy. And he hadn't let her down all night. They'd drifted into sleep and then he'd woken her, his lips on her breast, his fingers stroking her core, forcing her to orgasm again before she'd even been fully awake. She'd been like a wild thing, matching his demands with her own, responding to his every touch, his every kiss. No wonder she was exhausted; she'd never experienced anything like it before in her life. He'd played her like a violin and she'd enjoyed every second of it.

Ignoring the weakness in her legs, the discomfort between her thighs, she eased the cover off and slid out of the bed.

He flopped onto his back and threw one long, muscled

forearm across his eyes. Mel held her breath, letting it out only when she was sure his breathing remained deep and even.

The duvet had slipped down, revealing more of his chest. She studied the flat brown nipples nestled in the sprinkling of dark hair. Had she kissed them last night? The memory flashed back to her. Of course, she had.

Stop it, you ninny. Yes, it had been fantastic, but the guy was obviously a practised womaniser. Last night might have been something special for her, but she very much doubted it had been anything out of the ordinary for him. She certainly was not the first woman he'd taken to paradise—he knew the route there far too well. The smooth compliments, those sexy looks all evening—how many other women had he tried them on?

Then a thought struck her and she stiffened. Oh, no, he couldn't be, could he? Surely, she couldn't have made the same awful mistake twice. But she hadn't even asked. Why hadn't she asked?

Because it had been so long since she'd felt that pretty, that excited, that desirable. She'd decided to take what she wanted and hadn't thought about the consequences.

She bit her lip and tiptoed round the bed. The room was well heated but she shivered as she picked up the remnants of her underwear and dashed into the living room. Finding the robe she had discarded the night before, she put it on and went to the door of the suite.

She sent up a prayer of thanks when she spotted the brown-paper-wrapped package outside the door. It took her all of ten seconds to get dressed, keeping her ears peeled for any sound from the room next door. It took her a few frantic minutes more to find her damp shoes and her bag.

As she walked to the door she passed the table where the remnants of their meal still sat. The dirty plates and cutlery, the soured dregs of wine in smudged glasses, made it seem so sordid all of a sudden. Mel felt the tears well up in her eyes but ruthlessly held them back.

Obviously, she wasn't cut out for one-night stands, she realised. She'd be leaving a part of herself in this hotel suite, a part of herself with the man she'd made love to the night before with such passion, such intensity, such abandon. How long would it take, she wondered, for her to forget the feel of his arms around her? The soft whisper of his lips against her ear when he'd told her she was beautiful? The smell of him as they lay curled together and drifted off to sleep?

Opening her bag, she pulled out her purse. She only had ten pounds left inside. She smoothed it out, placed it carefully on the table. The least she could do was give him something towards the meal. He'd set the scene so perfectly.

Even though it had all been an illusion. It had been a magical night.

The feeling of loss staggered her as she left the suite, shutting the door silently behind her.

CHAPTER FOUR

'MEL, look at this, you are not going to believe it.'

Mel glanced up from her keyboard as Louisa perched on the edge of her desk and shoved a piece of printed card under her nose.

'What is it?'

Louisa wiggled the card. 'Read it and see.'

Mel took it, trying to look enthusiastic. Monday mornings were bad enough, but after a week of disturbed sleep Mel was starting to resent her job—and her best friend.

When Mel went to bed every night the same dream would wake her up. She couldn't seem to forget about that night and that man. And, indirectly, the whole impossible mess was Louisa's fault.

As Mel read the card the irony of the situation made her want to weep. She handed the invitation back to Louisa. 'So, Devlin's finally giving a press conference. The world can stop holding its breath. Wonderful.'

'Stop being such a grump, Mel,' Louisa said lightly. 'Honestly, you've been almost as bad this past week as you were after you kicked out that lying creep Adam.' Louisa shoved the invitation back under Mel's nose. 'Look closer.'

Mel sighed and took it. 'What am I supposed to be looking

for? All it says is that Louisa DiMarco of *London Nights* is invited to attend the—'

'Louisa DiMarco,' Louisa said triumphantly. 'Dark Knight have addressed it to me, personally.' She whipped the square of embossed card out of Mel's hand, stroked it lovingly. 'Isn't it exciting? I'm starting to make a name for myself. All the networking is finally paying off.'

'That's great, Louisa.' Try as she might, Mel couldn't quite raise the expected smile.

Louisa didn't seem to notice. Her grin was big enough for both of them. Crossing her long legs in front of her, she leaned back and fluffed her luxurious blonde hair. She laughed, the sound bubbly and excited. Mel's jaw tightened.

'Remember that silly business at The Ritz? To think we thought that guy was Devlin.'

'*We* didn't think that guy was Devlin,' Mel pointed out. 'You did.'

Louisa stopped playing with her tresses and gave Mel an innocent look. 'I can't believe you're still so annoyed about that, Mel. Nothing happened, after all. He didn't discover you. I was the one who ended up snogging Colin for no reason. And you lost my press card.'

'You lied to me,' Mel said, keeping her voice level and getting annoyed all over again. 'You told me the magazine was about to go under. I could have been done for breaking and entering.' That, as it turned out, had been the least of the perils that had awaited her.

Louisa waved the comment away with a swish of her perfectly manicured fingers. 'It was only a little white lie—and anyway I've apologised about a hundred times. I don't know what else you expect me to do.'

Make me the way I was before that night, Mel thought silently. Stop me from thinking about Jack Dempsey every minute of every day. Stop me from spinning stupid romantic dreams about something that meant nothing.

'I know.' Louisa leaned forward, an eager smile curving her lips. 'Why don't you come with me? The press conference is this afternoon. I'll square it with Dansworth. You need to get out of the office. We can grab lunch at that lovely little Italian deli on Charlotte Street. The venue's right across the road.'

Mel gave a weary sigh. 'I've got tons to do here. I haven't even finished reading the book I'm supposed to be reviewing. And Fletcher slapped me with a load of proofs about ten minutes ago.'

'Don't worry about Fletcher.' Louisa fluttered her eye-lashes and grinned. 'I'll get him to do his own proofs. Oh, come on, Mel.' She gave her a playful punch on the shoulder. 'You've been in a funk for months now. You've got to start snapping out of it some time.'

She already had once, Mel thought, and look what it had got her.

'You've read all Devlin's books,' Louisa continued. 'If you come, you can think of some good questions I can ask him. Use your imagination, Mel. This is exciting. We're going to be among the first people in the world to interview him.'

A tiny slither of excitement worked its way into Mel's dismal mood. She took the card from Louisa, ran her thumb down the embossed print. Maybe, Louisa was right. Maybe it was about time she stopped sulking and got on with her life—again.

'What do you say?' Louisa asked, hopefully.

Mel handed the invite back to Louisa, her lips tilting up. The smile felt unfamiliar, but surprisingly good. 'All right, why not?'

'That's more like it.' Louisa grinned back at her. 'You never know,' she added, stuffing the invite into her bag, 'Devlin might even be as gorgeous as that hunk at The Ritz.'

Mel certainly hoped not.

* * *

'Hello, ladies.' The preppie guy standing at the door of the fancy suite of offices in Charlotte Street held up his clipboard and gave Louisa a hopeful smile. 'Can I have your names?'

'Certainly,' Louisa said, giving the young man one of her you-can-dream-buddy smiles. 'I'm Louisa DiMarco and this is Carmel Rourke, my editorial assistant.'

The guy checked his list, gave it a tick and handed Louisa a badge with her name and the *London Nights* logo printed on it. 'Here you go, Louisa, you can go through, but I'm afraid Carmel's not down here. Only the select few are allowed in.'

Mel felt her enthusiasm dim as Louisa pinned on her badge. But then Louisa tucked her arm through hers and held on tight. 'I can't go in without Mel. Couldn't you check and see if it's okay? Please?'

The guy hesitated for about a second. 'Wait there a minute. I'll go ask my boss. Maybe we can work something out.' He slipped through the door with his clipboard.

'Honestly, Louisa,' Mel whispered. 'That pout ought to be registered as a lethal weapon.'

Louisa wiggled her eyebrows. 'I know. Let's see if it works. Gosh, look, he's back already.'

The guy rushed out again, beaming at Louisa. 'Boss said it's not a problem. You've got a front-row seat, by the way, Louisa.'

'Really!' Even Louisa seemed surprised at that bit of information.

'Yes,' he replied, his eyes going dreamy as he held the door for them. 'You must be a very special lady.'

Louisa smiled as she tugged Mel along beside her. 'You don't know the half of it,' she said, throwing him a kiss as they walked briskly down the hallway.

Mel laughed. 'There goes another poor sucker.'

* * *

The conference room was brightly lit and spacious, but packed so full of journalists, camera operators, lights and assorted sound and film equipment, Mel felt as if she were stepping into the black hole of Calcutta. At least twenty rows of seats had been crammed in facing a raised platform. The table on the podium had a couple of microphones, a jug of water and a rather sad bunch of flowers on it. A huge poster of Devlin's latest book cover adorned the wall behind the stage. The lurid red type and the image of a blood-drenched knife made a peculiar contrast with the sagging hothouse roses.

As she and Louisa jostled their way to the front of the room, Mel recognised many of the journalists in attendance. A few were jotting things into notepads, some were chatting together, but most were talking furiously into their mobile phones. All the British dailies were represented, but Mel also spotted reporters from *The New York Times, The Washington Post* and *Le Monde*. The BBC, ITV and Sky News had their cameras packed in at the front of the room.

The flutter of anticipation in Mel's chest grew to a steady hum. Devlin and his publicist ought to get an award. They'd pulled off the publicity stunt of the year. Having read all of Devlin's books, though, Mel wondered for the umpteenth time why the writer had gone to such lengths to up his profile like this. His dark, compelling writing style was good enough to stand on its own. He didn't need this sort of gimmick.

Louisa, being Louisa, walked straight to the front row and, sure enough, to Mel's silent astonishment, there was a seat right in the middle of the row with a reserved sign and Louisa's name on it.

Louisa turned to her and grinned. 'Go and sit in it, Mel. I'll get them to find me another.'

'But you can't. There's no room.'

Louisa winked. 'Watch and learn.'

As Mel perched on the seat, trying to ignore the disdain-ful looks of *The Times* journalist on one side and the *Time Out* guy on the other, she watched Louisa walk up to a burly security guard who stood next to the door behind the stage.

About twenty seconds later, the *Time Out* guy glared at them both as he was led to a seat two rows back.

Louisa settled next to her, unperturbed. 'Have you thought of any good questions to ask him?'

'I've thought of a few.'

'Brilliant.' Louisa reached into her bag and pulled out a pen and pad. 'Jot them down. They're bound to have a question and answer session. I can't wait.'

Mel had her head down and was busy scribbling when she heard a sudden furore as the journalists behind them stood up. The flash bulbs going off around her made it hard to concen-trate. She wrote as fast as she could, trying to ignore the clamour of shouted questions and the footsteps on the dais in front of them. Devlin must have entered the building, she thought with a smile.

'I don't believe it.'

Hearing the shock in Louisa's voice, Mel lifted her head. The pen dropped from her numb fingers as she focused on the man sitting right in front of her on the podium. He stared straight at her—the familiar blue of his irises colder and more brittle than shards of ice.

Her heart stopped and every single molecule of blood drained out of her face.

'I give you Devlin, ladies and gentlemen.' The pub-lisher's announcement reverberated in Mel's ears like a clap of thunder. 'The world's most mysterious mystery writer—and the biggest selling author worldwide for the last three years.'

Mel's heart finally began to pound again, the breath gushed out of her lungs. He still hadn't taken his eyes off her.

Shouted questions poured from the reporters around her. She ducked her head, scrambled to find her bag. She could feel her face blazing, her legs starting to shake. She absolutely had to get out of here before she threw up.

She shoved the pad and pen blindly at Louisa, who still looked astonished. 'Take this, I've got to go.'

'What? Wait.' Louisa gripped her arm as she tried to rise. 'What's wrong with you?' she hissed.

'I've got to leave,' Mel said, keeping her head down. Was he still staring at her? All she could hear was the clamour of questions being shouted over the publisher's introductory speech.

'Don't be ridiculous,' Louisa replied. 'Did you see who he is?'

The panic rising up Mel's throat started to choke her. 'Yes,' she whispered back, jerking her arm free.

'I'll take my first question from Louisa DiMarco of *London Nights* magazine.' The low, familiar rumble of his voice boomed out from the microphone above her.

Mel lifted her eyes to his. He was still watching her. In fact, the whole room was watching her. The noise quietened as the cameras turned onto Mel.

Louisa lifted two fingers and cleared her throat, looking truly perplexed for the first time in her life. 'That's great, thanks, Mr Devlin, I'm honoured.' Louisa waved her hand and the cameras swung round to her.

Devlin's brow furrowed, his eyes narrowed ominously as he continued to stare at Mel for a moment longer, then he switched his attention to her friend.

Mel forced her legs to straighten. As Louisa started to read out the question on the pad Mel pushed her way through the journalists who crowded round the podium. She got several odd stares but she didn't care.

'What's so bloody special about Louisa Dee-flaming-Marco?' she heard the *Time Out* guy moan as she stumbled past him.

Devlin's low voice, stiff with tension, ground out an answer to Louisa's question as Mel shoved open the door and rushed out into the corridor.

Mel had got about twenty paces down the hall when her stomach heaved. Spotting the ladies' toilet, she ran inside. Several painful minutes later, she walked out of the cubicle, her lunch now history. Catching a glimpse of herself in the washroom mirror, she cringed. Curls of chestnut hair dangled out of her pony-tail, while the dark shadows under her eyes could frighten small children at ten paces.

'Shoe salesman indeed,' she hissed at her reflection.

He'd lied to her, but, worse than that, he'd set her up.

Louisa's personal invite to the press conference. The specially reserved seat in the front row. It all made sense now. His plan had been to humiliate her. Her knees went a little weak. Was that why he'd seduced her, as well?

Devlin probably hated reporters; after all, they'd been hounding him for years.

Suddenly, it all made such perfect sense. The wine, the steak, the compliments, the whole candlelit seduction. He'd found her in his room and he'd seen an opportunity to get even. And she, like a stupid, romantic fool, had started flirting with him, encouraging him. She might as well have stripped naked in front of him. Forget might as well—she had.

She heard a storm of applause from the room down the hallway. The nausea gripped her stomach again. Had he intended to announce at the press conference what had happened between them?

While she'd been thinking about him constantly in the last week, waking up hot and sweaty in the middle of the night, beating herself up over whether there had been more to it than just incredible sex, he'd been laughing at her and planning to make a fool of her. Just like Adam. How could she have been such an idiot?

She pulled tissues out of the box on the counter top, blew her nose and wiped the drops of moisture from her eyes. They were not tears; she was not going to cry over that man. She tied the belt on her overcoat, noting with satisfaction that, while her knees were a bit wobbly and she still looked dreadful, her hands were steady.

Then Louisa burst through the door.

'There you are. You ninny. Why did you run out like that?' She dashed up to Mel, grabbed her upper arms. 'It was incredible. He's incredible. He answered all three of those questions you scribbled down. If you hadn't run out, I'm sure he would have answered more. He only took two questions after that. One from *The New York Times* and one from the BBC.' Louisa's eyes glowed with excitement. 'And he's even more mouth-watering up close.' Louisa finally wound down. 'Mel, what's wrong?'

Mel pulled her arms free, picked up her bag and slung it over her shoulder. 'Nothing's wrong. I felt a bit claustrophobic.'

She headed for the door, but Louisa blocked her way. 'Something's going on here. I know it is.'

Great, Louisa's skills as an investigative reporter kick in just in time to make things even worse. 'Nothing's going on, don't be silly.'

'He asked after you.'

'What?'

'The publisher asked me your name. He said Devlin wanted to know.'

'Please tell me you didn't tell him.' This could not be happening.

'Of course I did. Why wouldn't I?'

'Right, okay.' Mel straightened her shoulders, tried to feign indifference.

Louisa frowned. 'He found you in that room, didn't he?'

'No, he didn't.' Even Mel could hear the false squeak in her voice.

'Oh—my—God.' Louisa's eyes lit up like a beacon. She started flapping her hands. 'You slept with him.'

'What?'

'Don't lie. It's written all over your face.'

'It is not.' Mel had to force herself not to double-check in the mirror.

Louisa's grin got bigger. 'What's the matter with you? This is fantastic.' She couldn't have looked more excited if she were dancing a jig. 'He's as handsome as George Clooney, probably just as rich and he's got to be at least five years younger. How old is Gorgeous George anyway?' Her face fell, suddenly. 'He wasn't rubbish in bed, was he? Devlin, I mean.'

'No, he wasn't he—'

Mel cut herself off. Too late. Louisa was already whooping and clapping her hands.

'I knew it. I knew it. If it looks like a hunk, acts like a hunk, smells like a hunk, then it is a hunk.' She linked her arm with Mel's. 'Now, tell your auntie Louisa all about it. And don't spare any of the details. I'm woman enough to take it.'

Mel tugged her arm free. 'Will you shut up? I have not just won the lottery. He only seduced me because he thought I was you.'

Louisa considered the words for a moment, then shook her head. 'As much as my ego would love to believe that, Mel, it's not true. I put my best come-to-bed eyes on the whole time I was asking him those three questions and he didn't even smile. In fact, he hardly even noticed me.' Louisa's eyes twinkled mischievously. 'He was too busy watching you leave the room. And now we know why. God, Mel. You're such a dark horse. When are you going to see him again?'

'I'm not going to see him again. And will you stop behaving as if this was the romance of the century? Believe me, it's not. What I meant was, he thought I was a reporter. That's why he slept with me. That's why he gave you the invite to the press conference. The front-row seat. It was all a means of getting back at reporters.'

Louisa was speechless, for about ten seconds. 'You think he had sex with you as a punishment? Ooh, that's really kinky. I like it. Nothing like a bit of S and M to spice up a relationship.'

'It's not funny,' Mel said, glaring at her friend, although the sex as revenge thing was sounding a bit silly to her now too.

'Come on, Mel. I was only kidding. It's just, the idea that he slept with you because he doesn't like reporters is ridiculous. I know your confidence took a battering after what happened with Adam the creep—' her voice went low with sincerity '—but don't throw the hunk out with the bathwater. What makes you think Devlin wouldn't want to seduce you? You're funny, you're smart, you're clever and you're beautiful, Mel, when you make the effort, which, frankly, you haven't done often enough lately.'

Mel sighed. Defeated. Louisa was hopeless. But then, that was what she loved about her. For all her shortcomings, Louisa had a generous spirit and a generous heart—and she never believed in complicating fantasy with reality. Sometimes Mel wished she could do the same, but she couldn't, not any more. She'd grown up.

'Why don't we just say he's not my type, Lou, and leave it at that?' Seeing her friend was about to object, Mel tucked her arm back in Louisa's and led her to the door. 'I need a drink—preferably a two-litre margarita with enough tequila in it to make George Clooney sit up and beg.'

She didn't think her stomach would stand an alcoholic drink, but it made Louisa smile, as she had intended.

'I know the perfect place,' Louisa said. 'As long as you remember, George's mine.' But as they walked out the door her friend shook her head and sent Mel a rueful smile. 'Honestly, Mel. Talk about looking a gift horse in the mouth. You'd shove a stick of dynamite down its throat.'

CHAPTER FIVE

'I'VE got to go to the Ladies, drink up.' Louisa hopped off the barstool. 'I'm ordering another round on my way back.'

Mel took a sip from her tepid margarita. 'I don't want another. I've got to get home.'

'It's only six-thirty. You need to live a little.' Louisa picked her bag up and headed towards the toilets.

Mel watched her friend's long strides eat up the dark granite tiles of the snazzy Soho pub. A group of city types sitting at the other end of the dimly lit bar ogled Louisa as she strolled past.

No doubt she and Louisa would be fending them off soon when they got up the courage to come over. From the joking and slapping of backs that was going on as Louisa disappeared into the Ladies, Mel didn't think it would be a very long wait. She usually enjoyed watching Louisa in full flirt mode, but Mel didn't feel up to it tonight. She'd put herself through emotional hell in the last few days and she needed to get her life back on track. First on her to-do list was an early night.

Staring down at her margarita, Mel tried to visualise a hot bubble bath, a large bar of chocolate and her bed—with no one in it but her.

'Hello, Louisa.'

Mel's fingers tensed on the glass. Her head swung round.

'Or is it Carmel?' Cool blue eyes stared at her out of a tanned angular face she remembered only too well.

Terrific. 'What are you doing here?'

'Tracking you down, Cinderella, what does it look like?' His voice sounded amused, but the crinkles round his eyes were absent.

'I'm afraid you've wasted your time. I'm leaving.'

She put her hands on the bar to climb down but strong fingers clamped onto her wrist. Her heartbeat shot up at the contact.

'Think again, Cinders,' he growled. He didn't sound amused any more. Keeping a firm hold of her wrist, he shouted to the bartender. 'Bring me a bottle of Corona, buddy. The lady will have another margarita.'

The bartender nodded and walked off to fill their order.

'I don't want another drink,' Mel whispered furiously. 'I told you I'm leaving.'

She tugged her hand; his fingers tightened on her wrist.

'And I'm telling you, I didn't spend the last twenty minutes checking out the bars round here to have you skip out on me again without an explanation.'

'An explanation for what exactly?' How dared he look at her as if she were the guilty party?

'For the little disappearing act you pulled at the hotel. What else?'

'I don't owe you an explanation for that or anything else.' She tugged again, still no movement. 'Let go of my hand or I'll scream the place down.'

'No, you won't.' He climbed onto the stool next to her, his fingers still curled round her wrist. 'You're British. You'd as soon have your toenails pulled out with a pair of pliers as make a scene.'

She pulled harder. It still didn't budge. 'Yes, well, I'm willing to make an exception in your case and sacrifice my toenails.'

'Now that's a shame,' he murmured, the low timbre of his

voice reminding her of things she definitely did not want to be reminded of. 'Because, if I recall correctly, you've got real cute toenails.' He lifted her wrist off the bar and brushed the pulse point with his thumb. 'You still got that pretty pink polish on them?'

'That does it.' With the blush blazing in her cheeks, she jumped off the stool and pulled her hand hard. He let go and she stumbled back a step.

'Easy, now, Cinders. No need to fall at my feet.'

'Don't worry, I won't,' she snapped, trying to ignore the way her pulse was jumping like a jackrabbit being chased by a fox.

'Well, hello, Mr Devlin.'

Relief coursed through Mel. If Louisa had been a lifeboat on the *Titanic*, she couldn't have been happier to see her.

Devlin turned round. 'Hi. It's Louisa, isn't it? Great to meet you,' he said, the poster boy of politeness, and shook Louisa's hand.

'I'm impressed, you remembered.' Louisa smiled back at him as if they were the best of friends.

Mel blinked, sure she'd just slipped into an alternative reality.

'That'll be eight pounds fifty, mate,' the bartender said as he slid their drinks across the bar.

'Oh, fantastic.' Louisa beamed. 'Are you joining us for a drink, Mr Devlin?'

'Devlin will do.' He pulled his wallet out of the back pocket of his jeans and slapped a twenty-pound note on the bar. 'Louisa, I need to talk to your colleague in private. Order yourself another drink and we'll be back in a minute.' He scooped the bottle and the margarita off the bar with one hand. 'How does that sound?'

Mel gestured frantically behind his back, shaking her head at Louisa, but her friend just smiled sweetly at him. 'That sounds absolutely marvellous, Devlin,' she purred, giving Mel a none-too-subtle wink.

So much for Louisa the lifeboat, more like Louisa the flipping iceberg. Mel opened her mouth to object, but before she could decide who to lay into first Devlin gripped her upper arm and steered her towards one of the booths at the back of the pub.

He slammed the drinks on the table, splashing the margarita onto the shiny metallic surface. 'Sit down, Cinders.' So much for politeness.

Mel shrugged out of his grasp. 'Stop ordering me about,' she hissed, fisting her hands on her hips. 'Stop manhandling me. And stop calling me Cinders.'

'Sit. Down. Please.' He enunciated the words as if talking to a disobedient child.

Mel bristled, but noticed his glare was hot enough to melt steel. It occurred to her he was a man in a serious snit. Maybe a temper contest was not the way to go here.

She sat down.

Without asking, he pushed onto the seat beside her. His thigh nudged hers and she shifted away, creating as much distance as possible between them. She already knew physical contact with him was not good for her heart rate.

He rested one arm on the back of the bench seat and the other on the table, boxing her in. She'd forgotten how tall he was, how broad his shoulders were. She could hardly see past him. The faint smell of his aftershave brought back more unwanted memories.

'Do you mind not sitting so close to me, please?'

He gave a harsh laugh. 'I've been a lot closer to you than this, Cinders—and I didn't hear you complaining.'

The sarcastic nickname and the blatant insinuation in his eyes lit her temper back up like torch-paper. 'Well, I'm complaining now. And don't call me Cinders.'

'Why the hell not? I figure it fits.' His lips had twisted into what looked perilously close to a sneer. 'Wasn't she the woman who skipped out on the guy in the middle of the night?'

'Look, Prince Charming,' she said, layering as much sarcasm into her voice as he had. 'You were supposed to be a shoe salesman from Idaho, remember? So the way I see it we're even.'

How had she ever believed that whopper? she thought as she took in his long, powerful frame encased in black jeans and a dark blue jumper with a Ralph Lauren logo.

He swore under his breath, and swung round, resting both his arms on the table. He lifted the beer bottle. His Adam's apple bobbed as he took a long gulp. 'Okay,' he said, frustration edging his voice. 'Maybe we're even.' His eyes met hers. A lock of hair fell over his forehead and he scraped it back with an impatient hand. 'But I still want to know why you ran out on me.'

For a moment she saw something flicker in his eyes. Had she hurt him? But then it was gone and she felt silly for even thinking it. 'Why do you care?'

Okay, that tore it. Jack slammed the bottle back down on the table, making her jump. 'Don't do that female thing of answering a question with another question—just give me a straight answer.'

It was the least she owed him, he figured. The woman had turned him inside out and back again in the last week. The fact that looking at her now made him want to kiss her and throttle her at one and the same time only pushed him closer to the edge.

'I… It was morning,' she said. 'I had somewhere I had to go.' It wasn't the truth—he was sure of it when her eyes dipped to her lap.

'And what was the ten bucks for? Services rendered?' The bitterness churned inside him as it had when he'd found the money.

She flinched, her skin looking even paler than usual in the low light from the bar. 'It was all I had in my purse. I thought I ought to give you something, towards the meal and the laundry bill.' She stared at him. Hell, those eyes could cut a guy off at the knees. 'I didn't mean to insult you. If I did, I'm sorry for it.'

He felt the knot of tension that had been lodged in his gut all week start to loosen.

She picked her bag up and hooked it onto her shoulder before her eyes met his. 'If there's nothing more you need to ask me, I've got to go.'

It surprised him to realise there was a lot more he wanted to ask her. The real reason she'd run out on him, for starters. But what surprised him more was the realisation that he didn't want her to go. 'You haven't had any of your drink,' he said at last.

She fidgeted with the strap of her bag. 'Louisa will be wondering where I am.'

He glanced round towards the bar, spotted the Amazon holding court surrounded by a gang of eager young guys in business suits. 'Louisa looks like she's doing fine on her own.' He turned back, picked up the margarita glass and held it to her lips. 'Come on, one sip won't do you any harm.'

'All right.' She sighed, took the glass. The tip of her tongue darted out and licked the salt off the rim. An arrow of lust shot straight down to his crotch. He tensed. He was getting hard just watching her.

Mel saw the flash of heat as his gaze dropped to her lips, felt the instant response at her core. The effect he had on her was just as potent now as it had been a week ago, she realised with horror.

She needed to get out of here now, before she did something really stupid, again. The margarita glass hit the table with a thud. 'I really should be going.'

His eyes lifted to hers, but he didn't move. 'Running scared again, Cinders?'

The nickname and the teasing warmth in his eyes when

he said it made Mel's insides go all tingly. A traitorous blush crept up her neck. 'Just being smart,' she said, deciding there was no point in pretending she didn't know what he meant.

'Smart, huh?' He reached up, brushed his fingertip down her cheek.

'Yes, smart.' She pulled back, trying to ignore the tug of need as his hand fell away from her face. 'I think it's better not to let your hormones rule your head.'

'That's not the way you felt a week ago.'

What exactly was she supposed to say to that? 'Well, it's the way I feel now.'

'You wanna know what I think?'

She was sure she didn't, but she was finding it hard to breathe, let alone object.

'I think we should give it another shot.'

She couldn't have been more shocked if he had tipped the margarita on her head. Was he serious? 'I don't think so.'

'Why not? There was a hell of a connection between us that night.'

Exactly, she thought. That sort of explosive sexual chemistry was not the safe option. Which was what she needed in her life. Wasn't it?

'I really do have to go,' she said.

His eyes narrowed, but then he shrugged. 'Fine, run off again, if that's what you want.' Mel's shoulders relaxed a little. She needed to get out of here. She couldn't think straight with him so close to her.

He got up, but as she scrambled past him he snagged her arm. 'This isn't the end of it, you know.'

Why couldn't she stop trembling? 'What do you mean by that?'

'You're a smart girl.' His thumb stroked the inside of her elbow, making her quiver. 'I'm sure you can figure it out.'

Her breath released as he let go of her arm.

Mel wanted to run. She forced herself to walk, but she didn't look back once.

Jack kept his eyes on Mel as she rushed over to her friend, exchanged a few words and then left. He sat back down in the booth, picked up his beer and finished it in two long gulps.

Placing the bottle back on the table, he noticed her nearly full margarita. He touched the lip of the glass where her tongue had removed the salt.

He shook his head, glanced back at the exit. Something had happened to him a week ago. Something he didn't understand. He hadn't been able to get her out of his mind. He knew damn well it could only be lust. What else could it be? But whatever it was, she wasn't out of his system yet. And he wasn't out of hers either. He'd seen the way she'd looked at him a moment ago, felt the way she'd trembled when he'd touched her.

After she'd shot out of the press conference, he'd planned to track her down and give her hell. For lying to him about who she was—and for running out on him a week ago. He hitched a shoulder. Okay, so he'd lied to her too, but he'd had good reasons.

The minute he'd seen her again, though, he'd known it wasn't going to be that simple.

He gave a weary sigh. But how the hell had it got so complicated?

Why had his usual composure completely deserted him tonight? And why had she run out on him again?

His shoulders slumped as he dragged a tired hand through his hair.

Truth be told, it wasn't just the situation with the irresistible and infuriating Carmel Rourke that was bugging him. Not by a long shot.

The clamour of reporters and photographers this afternoon was the beginning of his own personal three-week nightmare. After two long years of begging, the PR people at Dark Knight had finally got him to agree to be at their disposal. Even with Christmas in less than a week, he knew they had book signings and press conferences in Paris, New York and LA lined up over the next couple of weeks. The thought of it made him tense. They'd even been talking about lining up a reporter from one of the glossy magazines to do a profile on him. Just what he needed right now, some snoop trailing around after him, asking him questions he had no intention of answering. At least they'd given him final approval on the name.

Jack blinked and sat upright. The thought hitting his brain like a bolt of lightning. A slow smile curved his lips.

Why not? Didn't someone once say misery loved company? If he was going to be in purgatory for the next few weeks, he couldn't think of a better person to share it with him.

CHAPTER SIX

'HEY, Mel, Dansworth wants to see you in her office, pronto.'

'Thanks, Jim.' Mel's stomach sank as she tapped the final line of her book review into the computer.

What now? All she needed was a dressing down from her boss to make this the perfect week. And it was only Wednesday.

She'd been feeling needy and confused and totally unsettled ever since her encounter with Devlin on Monday night. She turned off her screen. She must have replayed it a hundred times in her head since. The look on his face when he asked her why she ran out on him. The rough feel of his fingertip on her cheek. And then the ridiculous suggestion that they 'give it another shot'. For goodness' sake, they didn't know each other. In fact, she wasn't even sure they liked each other.

She was so stressed out, she'd actually lost weight. Whatever she did, she couldn't seem to get her mind clear of the man.

It hadn't exactly helped that in the last week the news media had been full of stories about him. As far as she could see the 'Mystery Novelist Comes Out of Hiding' lead was getting a bit old, but no one else seemed to agree. Only last night she'd had to leap up and turn the telly off when a piece about him had popped up. The fact that he hadn't given any other interviews or press conferences had probably helped stoke all the speculation. The man really knew how to milk as much publicity out of the whole situation as was humanly possible, she thought grimly.

She pulled the plain blue cardigan off the back of her chair and put it on. She had a feeling it was going to be frosty in Dansworth's office; it usually was. She and the editor did not see eye to eye. While Josephine Dansworth adored Louisa, Mel had never fitted in to the whole tabloid environment and she knew it. She didn't do frivolous and gossipy and her book reviews reflected that. No doubt her editor was going to tell her to 'sex up' her copy again. Mel's jaw tightened as she walked down the corridor to her boss's office.

Dansworth's door was ajar. Through it Mel could see a small blond man who looked vaguely familiar. She knocked on the frosted-glass panel. 'Mrs Dansworth, I understand you wanted to see me?' she said from the doorway.

The blond guy gave her an eager smile and stood up.

The older woman beckoned from her desk. 'Take a seat, Mel,' she said, a warm smile on her face. Mel blinked. Her boss had never, ever smiled at her before. 'Please sit down, gentlemen.'

Gentlemen? Mel turned to find a seat and spotted the other man, who had been sitting behind the door. Her pulse-rate started popping and heat hit her cheeks.

What was *he* doing here?

'Hello, Miss Rourke.' His eyes flickered with amusement as he gave her a challenging smile.

The only seat left in the small office was the chair next to him. Mel perched on the end of it and stared straight ahead at Dansworth. Maybe if she ignored him, he'd disappear.

'Mel,' Dansworth said, still grinning like a loon, 'I have amazing news for you.'

Mel remained silent, sure she could feel his eyes boring a hole in her back. What was this all about? And why did she have the feeling it was not going to be good?

'As I'm sure you know, this is Mr Devlin,' Dansworth announced as if she were introducing the President of America.

Forced to acknowledge him, Mel turned and gave him a stiff nod. Why was he smiling like that?

'And this is Mr Eli Thorn, the managing director of Dark Knight,' Dansworth continued.

'Hi, Mel. It's great to meet you,' the blond guy said in a thick New York drawl. She shook the hand he offered. She remembered him now. He was the publisher who had introduced Devlin at the press conference.

'Mr Devlin and Mr Thorn have decided that they'd like a reporter from *London Nights* to cover Mr Devlin's up-coming book tour—and your name has been mentioned.'

Mel swallowed. 'I beg your pardon?' Surely, she couldn't have heard that right.

'Mel, you'll be travelling with Mr Devlin and his PR people for the next few weeks. The idea is to do a profile of Mr Devlin and his work.' Dansworth's voice bubbled with enthusiasm. Her face glowed with excitement. 'You'll have unprecedented access to him. It's a marvellous opportunity for the magazine and for you as a reporter.'

Mel stared at her boss. Was the woman completely mad? Hadn't she missed the obvious here? 'But, Mrs Dansworth, I'm not a reporter. I'm an editorial assistant.'

Dansworth waved the remark away and gave a false little laugh. 'Don't be silly, Mel, of course you're a reporter.' She shot Mel a pointed look before pasting the insincere smile back on her face. 'Mr Devlin has requested you especially for this assignment.'

I'll just bet he has, Mel thought, suddenly feeling trapped. Her temper kicked in. So this was what he had meant by it wasn't over. Of all the arrogant, manipulative… Well, he wasn't going to get away with it.

'I'm sure Louisa would do a much better job,' Mel said, keeping her voice as light as she could.

'I don't want Louisa. I want you.'

Mel turned sharply. He looked relaxed and cocky, leaning back in his chair, his long legs crossed at the knee and those cool blue eyes fixed on her.

'Well, you can't have me, Mr Devlin.'

His lips quirked. Mel felt the heat in her cheeks reach boiling point. Of course, they both knew he'd already had her in practically every way possible. One dark brow lifted provocatively, as if he was challenging her to deny it. Mel's heartbeat thumped in her chest.

'Don't be ridiculous, Mel. Of course you'll do it,' Dansworth said brightly, oblivious to the tension humming in the air.

Mel tore her eyes away from Devlin and turned back to her boss. The fierce look on Dansworth's face belied the cheery tone of her voice.

'The details have already been arranged,' Dansworth said. 'The magazine will set up an expense account for you for the duration of the tour. Mr Thorn's PR people will be giving us details of the dates in the next few days so we can book your flights. Mr Devlin has very graciously agreed to let you stay in his residences in Paris and New York, but we'll be—'

'What?' Mel blurted out, horrified.

Dansworth glanced up from her spiel and frowned. 'It'll give you the opportunity to see Mr Devlin on his home turf, so to speak.' She threw Devlin an ingratiating smile. 'Unfortunately, he's refused to let a photographer in, so you'll have to paint a picture for our readers with your description, Mel.'

Mel's hands began to tremble; she clutched them together in her lap. She could not stay with him. This was a disaster. Her mind began to root around for any possible excuse.

'But it's Christmas in four days, Mrs Dansworth. My family will be expecting me at home.'

'This is your career, Mel.' Dansworth bit the words out, her tone now tight with annoyance. Mel knew her boss wanted to say a lot more but was restraining herself in front of their audience. 'I'm sure your family will understand.'

'The schedule's not totally fixed yet,' Eli Thorn piped up from his corner. Mel had forgotten he was even there. 'I'm sure we can work something out.' The publisher gave her a weak smile, looking confused.

No doubt he was wondering why an editorial assistant from a second-rate London rag wasn't jumping at the chance to cover the story of the year. But, at this stage, Mel didn't care how unprofessional or ridiculous she looked. She didn't want to be a reporter and she definitely didn't want to spend the next two to three weeks in close proximity to a man who affected her the way the man sitting next to her did. But short of handing in her notice, which she couldn't afford to do, it was beginning to look as if she wasn't going to be given a choice.

'Why don't I take you out to dinner this evening, Ms Rourke?'

Mel heard the cell door slam shut at the sound of Devlin's voice from behind her. She turned to stare at him.

'We can sort out our…' he paused, the creases round his eyes playing havoc with Mel's heart rate '…our working relationship.'

'What do you mean you don't want to do it? Are you nuts? Every reporter in the whole country…' Louisa stopped to take a breath '…actually, in the whole world, would die for this story. What's the matter with you?'

'You know very well what's the matter, Lou.' Mel sighed, toying with the grilled goat's cheese sandwich that sat untouched on her plate in the crowded Dean Street diner. 'For starters, I'm not a reporter.'

'Don't be daft,' Louisa said, taking another hearty bite of her own sandwich. She swallowed. 'You may not be a reporter, but you are a writer, Mel. Your book reviews are brilliant.' She took a quick sip of her cappuccino. 'You could write a fantastic profile on him, you know his work inside out. This could be your chance to catch the eye of all those posh magazines you've been sending your stuff to.' Louisa propped her elbows on the table. 'You could write a silly puff piece for Dansworth—that's all she really wants anyway. I'll help you with that. But once that's published you could write a proper piece about the man himself and what makes him tick. Devlin is the hot celebrity property at the moment. I mean, look at the guy: he's gorgeous, successful, mysterious—and you've got exclusive access to him.'

Mel shook her head. Why was Louisa being deliberately dense? 'Louisa, I don't want to do this. And you know very well the work side of it isn't the main reason.'

'So you slept with him. So what?'

Mel rolled her eyes. Why on earth had she thought Louisa would understand?

'Louisa, hasn't it occurred to you how suspicious this is? Out of all the big-name reporters—the real journalists—he could have picked, he asks for some complete nobody from a local magazine who's never written an article in her life to do his profile.'

'Okay, so he picked you because he slept with you,' Louisa said, undeterred. 'Can't you see how romantic that is? He's tracked you down, gone public with his real identity and laid the story of the century in your lap, all so he can see you again.'

Mel gave a harsh laugh, the burning in her chest almost painful. How could Louisa be so experienced with men and yet so naïve? 'We're not Romeo and Juliet, Lou. He's playing games. I think I insulted him when I walked out on him. I bet no woman's ever said no to him before. He sees me as some sort of silly challenge. This is all about the chase; once he's caught me again that'll be the end of it.'

'How do you know that?'

'He's the type. Believe me, I know,' Mel said with conviction.

'Rubbish. You don't know any such thing.'

Mel stiffened, surprised by Louisa's emphatic tone.

'You don't know what type he is because you don't know him at all,' Louisa continued, pointing an accusatory finger at Mel. 'And that's the real problem.'

Mel opened her mouth, but couldn't think of a thing to say.

'You know what your problem is, Mel. You're scared. Ever since you found out about Adam, you've been afraid to take a chance.'

Mel was dumbfounded. Where was all this coming from? Her friend had never talked to her like this before. Louisa had been her greatest supporter through that awful time. Why was she changing her tune now?

Louisa's eyes softened. 'Adam Harrington was a big fat creep. So what? He's history now. Don't you think it's about time you moved on? It's been nearly a year since you sent him packing, you know.'

Had it really been that long? 'I don't see what Adam's got to do with any of this,' Mel said, bewildered, but the protest sounded feeble.

Louisa leaned across the table, squeezed Mel's hand. 'Look, forget about Adam, okay. I've just got one question to ask you. Did you enjoy yourself that night at The Ritz with Mr Sex-on-a-Stick?'

'But I don't even know—' Mel began.

'Uh-uh.' Louisa wagged a finger at her, cutting off the protest in mid-stream. 'No evasions, no qualifications, no excuses and absolutely no buts allowed—unless we're talking about tight, squeezable male ones.' She wiggled her eyebrows suggestively. 'Answer the question, Mel. How was it for you, carnally speaking?'

Mel sighed. Who was she kidding? Just thinking about that night was making the heat coil low in her belly. 'Carnally speaking?' The memories she'd been struggling to suppress for over a week burst back into her brain. 'It was incredible.' She let out a slow breath. 'I've never felt so fantastic, so ful-filled, so—'

'You better stop there.' Louisa held her finger back up. 'That look in your eyes is starting to make me moist.'

Mel laughed, then sobered. Reliving the wonders of that night would not solve the problem. 'The point is, Louisa, it was just sex. I figured that out as soon as I woke up the next morning.'

'No, Mel.' Louisa shook her head. 'The point is it was great sex and you panicked the next morning.'

'Of course, I panicked. I didn't even know the guy.'

'Fair enough. So now you get to know the guy. He's given you the opportunity on a platter.'

'I don't think his motives for inviting me on this book tour were quite that pure,' Mel said, remembering the smoulder-ing look Devlin had given her at the Soho pub when he'd sug-gested they 'give it another shot'. She was certain getting to know her in anything other than the biblical sense was not on his agenda.

Louisa picked a crisp up from her plate and popped it in her mouth. 'Fine, so he's a bloke; his motives are probably less than pure. So what?' She shrugged. 'Let's face it, men's minds work in very simple ways—especially if fantastic sex is involved or is likely to be involved again.' She wiped her fingers with her napkin, dropped it back on the plate. 'The thing is, Mel, you've got as much power here as he does—why aren't you making the most of it?'

'How do you figure that?' Mel was intrigued, she realised, despite herself. She had felt powerless so far and Louisa was right—she hated feeling powerless after what had happened with Adam. Was that the real reason she found the situation with Devlin so hard to cope with? Because she couldn't control it?

'He wants you, Mel. And you want him. Why not use that to get to know him better? He may turn out to be a jerk. He may not. But what exactly have you got to lose? Whatever happens you'll have spent several weeks being escorted round the word's most glamorous cities by a guy who can give you multiple orgasms. It's what's called a no-brainer?'

'I don't know,' Mel said. Could it really be that easy? Could she just let herself go and see what happened?

'Tell you what,' Louisa said, taking her bag off the back of her chair. 'You're going out with him tonight, right? A business dinner?' She raised her eyebrows.

'Well, that's what he called it.' Mel smiled, the prospect of tonight's dinner not quite so daunting any more. 'He's picking me up at seven at my flat.'

Louisa stood up. 'I bet you anything he'll take you somewhere swish. You know, to show off.'

Mel groaned as they pressed through the crowd of people waiting for a seat. Louisa was probably right. And it would immediately put her at a disadvantage. She didn't do swish; she didn't have the finances for it. Once they were out of the busy café, Louisa threaded her arm through Mel's and squeezed.

'Don't start panicking again. I know a little place in Covent Garden which sells designer stuff second hand. How about we go down there after work and find the perfect outfit?' Louisa winked. 'You can start getting to know him and knock his socks off in the process.'

Ominous grey clouds hung over Oxford Street as people rushed about looking tired and harassed from the horrors of shopping so close to Christmas. But as Mel pushed through the crowds, her arm linked in Louisa's, the confusion and worry that had been dragging her down for over a week began to lift, ever so slightly.

The promise of what was to come, tonight and over the weeks ahead, didn't seem quite so scary any more. In fact, it might even be a little bit exciting.

CHAPTER SEVEN

MEL jumped at the sound of the doorbell and nearly poked her eye out with the eyeliner pencil. 'Ow!'

Taking two careful breaths, she grabbed some tissues from the box on the vanity and repaired the damage. Stuffing more tissues into the diamanté clutch purse Louisa had lent her, she took one more long look at herself in the bathroom mirror. Did she look like a sleek, sophisticated and go-getting investigative reporter—or did she look like a lowly book reviewer dolled up as one?

The doorbell buzzed again.

Mel glanced at her watch. Only six-fifty. Devlin was ten minutes early. Was that a good sign? Or a terrible one?

With unsteady hands, she smoothed the simple but impossibly chic bronze silk dress Louisa had insisted she buy for tonight's so-called business dinner.

The bubble of excitement, which had been building since Louisa had given her the pep talk to end all pep talks that afternoon, had burst about an hour ago. Now, she was simply a quivering bundle of nerves.

Another loud buzz from the doorbell.

Stop being an idiot and go answer the door.

The delicate drop earrings she wore sparkled, catching Mel's eye as she passed the little mirror hung by the front door. She could see his tall frame through the bevelled glass. And stopped dead. Her heartbeat pounded in her ears. A chestnut curl fell in front of her face and she pushed it away. Louisa had spent close to an hour before she left artfully arranging Mel's unruly hair.

'He'll be desperate to have it falling down into his hands all evening. It makes a statement,' Louisa remarked as she pinned and twirled.

'What? That I'm easy,' Mel shot back at her, suddenly feeling like a lamb being shoed towards the slaughterhouse.

Well, if she'd been nervous then, she was practically a basket case now. Suppose he was standing on the other side of the door in jeans and a T-shirt? She'd look ridiculous in this get-up. Oh, stop it. Mel evened her breathing and pulled her stomach in. For goodness' sake, she'd already done the hard part—he'd seen her naked. All she had to do tonight was get to know him a little. How hard could that be? Straightening her back, she walked the last few feet to the door and swung it open with a confidence she didn't quite feel.

Jack sucked in a breath at the vision in front of him. His heart slammed to a stop, then started beating again in double time. She looked stunning. The simple but seductive wisp of a dress hinted at rather than hugged her curves, but left him in no doubt as to just how soft and sexy she was underneath. Of course, he already knew how good she felt, how good she looked naked. But somehow this subtle reminder made the memory all the more potent. She'd done her hair up in some clever little arrangement that looked as if it were held up by will-power alone. His hands fisted in his pockets. He could remember dragging his fingers through the soft, fragrant mass of curls only too well. He forced his gaze to her face. Her green eyes, accented with a dash of dark, sultry make-up, watched him. She was probably expecting him to say something about her appearance, but for the first time ever his tongue wouldn't cooperate. He'd spent a lifetime complimenting women, but he couldn't think of a single thing to say.

He cleared his throat. 'Hi,' he said, his voice cracking like an awkward teenager on his first date.

'Hello,' Mel replied. Thank you, God, he had a suit on. Charcoal-grey and perfectly fitted to his wide shoulders. The simple white shirt underneath was open at the neck revealing a few tantalising wisps of chest hair. His eyes had widened when she'd opened the door but he hadn't commented on her appearance, which could only be a good thing. Surely.

'Would you like to come in for a minute?' she said, holding the door open. 'I need to get my coat.'

'Sure.' He stepped into the hallway behind her, making the small space feel even pokier.

'Did you have any trouble finding the place?' she asked, reaching into the hall closet for her woollen coat.

'No, but I thought I might have to commit murder to get a parking space.'

'I'm afraid they're like gold dust round here.' She turned back to him, her coat gripped in her hands. 'If I'd known you were driving I would have told you not to bother.'

'No bother. I like a challenge.' With his eyes intent on hers, she got the impression he wasn't talking about parking any more. 'Here.' He took the coat out of her hands. 'Let me.'

He held it up as she slipped her arms into the sleeves. The satin lining felt cool against her bare skin and made her shiver. His hands settled on her shoulders. He was so close she could smell him, the musky scent that was uniquely his.

'We better get going,' she said, nerves quickening her voice.

He smoothed the coat over her shoulders. 'Yeah,' he mumbled behind her and lifted his hands at last.

She picked up the purse from the small table beside the

door. The black leather heels Louisa had picked out for her clicked against the parquet flooring of the outside hall. As she locked the heavy oak door she saw him bury his hands back into the pockets of his trousers.

They walked down the darkened staircase together and his palm settled on the small of her back. It seemed to burn through the heavy wool, making her more aware of him than ever. She forced herself to steady her breathing again and repeated Louisa's assertion in her head. She had the power here. All she had to do now was figure out how to use it.

It was a good ten-minute walk to his car. The frigid wind made Mel huddle inside her coat and curse Louisa for the heels, which found every available crack in the pavement. His fingers gripped her elbow when her foot caught again and she stumbled.

'You okay?'

'Yes, it's these shoes—they don't go with London pavements.'

He glanced down at her feet. 'They do go with those legs, though,' he said, his eyes a deep, smoky blue in the light from the street lamp.

Mel felt the blush hit her cheeks and looked away, but was only too aware of his fingers on her arm as they walked the rest of the way to his car in silence.

Low-slung, sporty and shiny black, the car looked fast and dangerous. It suited him, she thought as he clicked the locks and held open the passenger door. She settled into the leather bucket seat. The car looked brand-new and, although she had no idea of the make, was probably hideously expensive. She pulled her coat a little tighter before fastening her seat belt.

The seat creaked as he sat beside her and slammed his door. She could just detect his aftershave above the scent of the new leather. What was it about the subtle smell that sent all her senses reeling?

He turned on the ignition and the engine's soft purr was followed by a blast of heat and Nina Simone's soulful, seductive voice.

'Nina work for you?' he asked.

'Yes,' she murmured. In fact, it was one of her favourite songs, but she didn't say so. Even though she'd been as intimate as was humanly possible with this man, telling him about her taste in music seemed too personal somehow.

He drove confidently, manoeuvring the powerful car through the Wednesday rush-hour traffic as if he were at Daytona.

'I booked us a table at a little place near here. The food's great. I hope you're hungry?' he said as the car cruised past the imposing, Georgian grandeur of Holland Park Avenue.

'I'm always hungry,' she said and bit her lip. Way to go, Mel. That sounded really sophisticated.

He chuckled, the sound rough and sexy. 'Good. I like a lady with an appetite.'

He was doing that *double entendre* thing, she thought, and tensed. Don't get carried away. This was a business dinner, plain and simple. She wasn't making any decisions yet. And she definitely wasn't jumping straight back into bed with him before she knew him a whole lot better. No matter what Louisa said.

The 'little place' he had booked turned out to be one of the swankiest restaurants in London, Mel discovered as he pulled into a parking space outside.

'You got us a table, here? Tonight?' Mel couldn't hide her amazement as she stepped out of the car. The Belvoir was strictly a 'special occasion' venue. She'd been there once before for her parents' thirtieth wedding anniversary and they'd booked a month in advance.

'Sure.' He shrugged. 'They had a late cancellation.'

'Was that before or after you told them who you were?'

'Hey, don't knock it,' he said as he slammed her car door. 'There ought to be some perks for getting hounded out of hiding.'

He put his hand on her back and steered her towards the restaurant. As Mel gave her coat to the hat-check girl and they were led down the curved, wrought-iron stairs to the restaurant's world-famous cellar dining rooms, Mel wondered about the offhand comment.

Was that how he really felt? That he'd been forced to reveal himself to the media. Was it possible the whole 'mystery man' thing hadn't been a publicity stunt after all?

Their table was situated in one of the dimly lit alcoves The Belvoir was renowned for. The ornately carved oak chairs and table, the wax-dripped candle in its decorative pewter holder and the lush velvet curtains draped over the entrance to the booth made it look as if it had been transplanted from the elf kingdom in *The Lord of the Rings*. Mel's confidence slid up a notch as she settled into her seat and the male diner in the booth opposite flicked his eyes down her dress. At least the calf-length, bias-cut silk sheath made her look the part.

She took the menu and the waitress reeled off a list of mouth-watering specials. While Devlin concentrated on the young woman's well-rehearsed spiel, Mel took the opportunity to study him in the shadowy light of the booth. He must have shaved before coming out, because there wasn't a hint of his usual five o'clock shadow. He would have looked sleek and sophisticated, every inch the rich, pampered bachelor but for the small crescent-shaped scar on his cheek, the tough, stubborn chin and the way his pitch-black hair, a little too long, curled against the white collar of his shirt. No wonder the press hounded him. With those movie-star looks and that tantalising air of inscrutability about him, who could blame them?

He turned back to her as the waitress left and caught her watching him. His eyebrow rose. Mel forced herself not to look away.

'How about we order first?' he said. 'Then we can talk about the tour.'

The words were businesslike, abrupt almost, but she knew she'd rattled him somehow.

'That works for me,' she said, unable to resist a small smile as she bent her head to study the menu.

After they had picked their starters and entrées—Mel choosing off the menu, because she couldn't remember a single one of the specials—the sommelier appeared to fuss over the chilled bottle of Chablis Devlin had ordered.

Mel sipped the dry white—and tried not to think about the last time she and Devlin had shared a bottle of wine. From the way he was looking at her over the rim of his glass, she had a feeling he might be remembering it too. The knowledge seemed to hang in the air between them.

'So where are we going on the book tour?' she asked.

He put his glass down, a smile tugging at his lips. 'You're coming?'

'Did I have a choice?' she replied, oddly flattered by the obvious pleasure in his voice.

'Choice is overrated,' Jack said, the surge of relief surprising him.

Then again, it wasn't the first surprise of the night.

He'd been ready for tantrums this evening, certainly some sulking. Had actually been looking forward to sparring with her—and getting her to admit that there was a lot more between them than a book tour. He'd got a real kick out of watching her in her editor's office that afternoon—her back ramrod-straight and her eyes determined to look at anything and everything but him. The effect he had on her must be pretty potent, he'd decided. Or she wouldn't be so determined to avoid him.

But she hadn't sulked. She didn't even seem all that annoyed about the way he'd manoeuvred her into this. He should have been pleased, but instead it made him feel a little uneasy.

But when she sipped her wine, the memories from that night surged through him like a hard, heady shot of adrenaline. He remembered the way she had flirted with him—soft and sweet and sexy as hell. And he wanted her to do it again. So he ignored his confusion and concentrated on the fact that she was going to be by his side for close to three weeks straight. He had every intention of taking as much advantage of that fact as was humanly possible.

'I've agreed to signings in Paris, New York, LA and the last stop's back in London.' He paused as the waitress slipped their appetisers in front of them, picked up his knife and fork. 'I've gotta do a Q and A in New York too, but that's it.'

'How many signings are you doing in each city?' Mel asked, spreading her trout terrine on a delicate slice of toasted rye bread.

He looked up from his plate. 'Just the one.'

'When do we leave?'

'Day after Christmas. We should be back in London around January tenth.'

The toast stopped halfway to her mouth. 'But that's over two weeks. And you're only doing…' she counted up the cities he'd mentioned '…three signings and a Q and A.'

He put down his fork, picked up his wineglass. 'That's right. I don't like to rush things—usually.'

She could see the teasing sparkle in his eyes. What exactly did he think they were going to be doing the rest of the time? Probably better not to go there, she decided.

'Anyway—' his lips curved in a provocative smile '—it'll give you more time to work on the profile.'

God, he was loving this. He obviously thought he had her right where he wanted her.

'Oh, yes, I almost forgot,' she said sweetly. 'I'm supposed to be finding out all your deep, dark secrets, aren't I, Mr Devlin?'

The smug smile still tugged at his lips. 'Call me Jack,' he said. 'No point us acting like we're strangers.'

'Sorry, I didn't know Jack was your real name.'

'The surname and the job were the only things I faked that night.' His eyes fixed on hers. 'In case you were wondering.'

'Oh, so you are from Idaho, then?' she said, pretending not to notice his insinuation.

He chuckled. 'Okay, you got me there. I don't exactly come from Idaho either.'

'Where do you come from? Exactly.'

His brow furrowed, ever so slightly. 'Around,' he said, dryly.

'Hmm, not exactly specific, are you?'

He shrugged and carried on eating his starter.

'Actually, Jack, I'm more interested in finding out why you booked into The Ritz under a false name.' She paused for effect. 'And why you kept your identity secret for so long.'

That wiped the smile off his face. 'You asking that on or off the record?'

'Off the record only exists in Hollywood movies, Jack. There's no such thing when you're dealing with a reporter,' she replied, enjoying the way his eyes narrowed. He didn't need to know that she was much more interested in finding out the answer to her question for herself than for the magazine article. 'I thought you knew that.'

'Right.' He dumped the forkful of lobster risotto back onto his plate. 'I kept a low profile because I wanted to be judged on what I write, nothing else. Identity's not important.'

'You were an unknown when you published *The Whisper Kill*,' she said, mentioning his first book. 'What else would you have been judged on?'

'Devlin is my real name,' he said, tightly. 'I didn't keep my identity secret, I just didn't advertise it.'

She'd really hit a nerve, she realised. 'Yes, but you did make yourself impossible to find. You wouldn't let your agent or your publisher release any details about you. You didn't have a bio in your books, you didn't attend any awards ceremonies, refused to do publicity, and—' she pushed her plate away '—you always kept one step ahead of the reporters. Why don't you just admit that you played the media game brilliantly and leave it at that?'

'Okay, if that's the way you want it.'

The minute he'd said it, Mel knew something was off. He'd acquiesced too easily.

'That's not it either, is it?' she said, watching him.

He didn't reply, just frowned.

'It wasn't a publicity stunt, was it?' she said softly, thinking out loud as his frown deepened. Then what he'd said earlier in the evening came back to her. 'You were in hiding. You said so yourself.'

He cursed. 'You're not going to put that in print, are you?'

'What do you have to hide, Jack?' she said softly, desperate to know the truth.

Jack almost groaned, but managed to stop himself. Maybe the next three weeks weren't going to be quite so easy after all. The plan had been to seduce her, get her back in his bed again where he wanted her, not have her dig up things about him that he'd spent his whole life running away from and then broadcast them to the world.

What exactly had he got himself into? And why, knowing how dangerous she might be, did he still want her so much?

'What the hell could I have to hide?' The words snapped out before he could stop them. He regretted the lapse when her eyes softened.

'I don't know, Jack. It must be important, though, if you'd go to such lengths,' she murmured.

The waitress stepped up to the table and took their plates away, but Jack kept his eyes on Mel. She dipped her head to smooth the napkin on her lap. Was that sympathy he'd seen in her eyes? And if it was, what was it for? She didn't know a thing about him. Nobody did. The heat she stirred inside him and the fact that she was a professional snoop were only part of the problem. That look she'd given, of sympathy, of trust, had almost made him want to tell her the truth, and if he did something like that, he might as well go to the nearest nut house and lock the door himself.

He forced what he hoped was a wry smile to his lips. 'You know, for someone who's not supposed to be a real reporter, you're doing a very good job of it.'

She should have pressed. That was what Louisa would have done—or any real reporter worth their salt. But Mel had seen the flash of anguish in his eyes before he'd been able to mask it—and she couldn't do it.

'Is that why you wanted me to do this job?' she asked carefully. 'Because you thought I wouldn't do it properly?'

'You know why I wanted you for this job,' he said. 'And it doesn't have a thing to do with any magazine article.'

The sudden intensity in his eyes, the deep, molten blue of his gaze, made Mel's heartbeat stutter, her skin feel warm and unbearably sensitive.

She nodded, not quite able to speak.

His lips curved and he leaned back in his chair, looking relaxed again and in control. 'I'm glad we got that straight,' he said.

No doubt about it, arrogance suited him even more than that fast, flashy sports car.

But the arrogance wasn't nearly as appealing as the vulnerability she sensed lay behind it. Anticipation welled up inside Mel as the waitress placed their entrées on the table with a flourish. The butterflies swooped about in her stomach like buzz bombers, but she knew she wasn't scared any more.

He was still watching her, a cocky smile on his impossibly handsome face.

She took a deep breath, let it out on a breathy sigh. 'Okay, Jack, so now we both know where we stand. The next few weeks should be quite an adventure.'

His teeth flashed in a quick grin. Lifting the bottle from its cooler, he splashed wine into her glass. 'Now, that's something I can drink to.'

He raised his glass, clinked it against hers. 'Here's to our trip. I figure it's going to be a wild ride.'

He didn't play his advantage for the rest of the meal, and for that Mel—and her stomach—were grateful. He kept the conversation light and funny. The man certainly knew how to flirt. Mel found herself relaxing and enjoying the attention. She asked a few pertinent questions about his books, which he answered with a complete lack of vanity. When she asked where his ideas came from, though, she hit a brick wall.

'That's a question all writers hate,' he said.

'Why?' She lifted her coffee to her lips.

'A good idea's like good sex. Once you get it, you should enjoy it—but if you analyse it to death you'll ruin it.'

She put her cup down gently. 'I see.' What did he mean by that?

'Hey, Cinders.' He covered her hand with his, gave it a quick squeeze. 'Don't look so shocked. I just figured you should know right off. If anything else happens between the two of us. And I'm hoping it does. I'm not looking for anything more.'

Mel blinked in surprise. Why would he think she was looking for more? 'It's nice of you to be so concerned,' she said, drawing her hand out from under his, 'but I can look after myself, Jack.' At least, she'd do her best. 'And I wouldn't count your chickens yet—good-sex-wise.'

* * *

Jack could have kicked himself. What the hell had he said that for? He'd never felt the urge before to warn off a woman he was hitting on. In fact, it was about the dumbest thing he'd ever done.

But somehow, even though he kept reminding himself she was a hard-headed reporter out for a big story, it didn't seem to fit. He'd read the book reviews she'd done of his work. She was a smart, clever writer, but what had surprised him was the depth of understanding there too. She'd let him off the hook earlier, when she could have got a nice juicy quote for her article. And he couldn't figure out why.

'Look, can we forget I said that?' He scraped his hair back from his brow. Changing the subject now would probably be a good idea, before he dug himself in any deeper. 'So where do your family live? You're with them for Christmas, right?'

'Mum and Dad live in Chiswick in West London. We always have a big family get-together there every year.'

'You looking forward to it?'

'Oh, yes.' Her eyes glowed with enthusiasm. 'I love it. All my brothers will be there with their families. It'll be fun.'

He should have talked about this sooner. He'd never seen her so open. '*All* your brothers? How many have you got?'

'Four of them, all older than me. Believe me, I wanted to murder them all when I was growing up. But it's lovely seeing them now. And all their wives and girlfriends are great,' she babbled on, warming to her subject. 'Christy and Meg are the only ones to have kids so far, but they had their second daughter six months ago, so that's been a big help evening out the testosterone overload. What will you be doing on Christmas Day?' she added brightly.

'Huh? Me?' He picked up the pot of coffee on the table, poured himself another cup. 'Packing, I guess. We're leaving for Paris the day after.'

'But won't you be celebrating with someone? Friends? Family?'

He hitched a shoulder. 'Nah. I'll hang out at the hotel.'

'But that's terrible. You can't be on your own on Christmas Day?'

Maybe it was talking about the great big family party at her Mum and Dad's place, or the wine making her melodramatic. But somehow the thought of him being alone in his hotel suite seemed unbearably sad to Mel.

'Sure I can. I don't really do Christmas,' he said.

'Are you Jewish or something?'

He laughed, sipped his coffee. 'No, it's just not a big deal for me. Never has been.'

What about when you were a child? she thought, but didn't ask. She had a feeling he wouldn't give her an answer. 'Why don't you come over to ours? My dad and Ty always cook enough to feed an army of starving rugby players.'

'Who's Ty?'

'He's my second oldest brother. He's a chef. And don't change the subject. Will you come?'

'Won't your folks be mad if a stranger turns up on their doorstep on Christmas Day?'

'Well, we're not exactly strangers, are we?' she said, neatly turning his own words back on him. 'And everyone would be thrilled to meet you. All my brothers are fans of your stuff.'

'I don't know…'

'Please come.' She didn't know why, but suddenly it seemed vitally important to Mel that he say yes.

CHAPTER EIGHT

JACK DEVLIN stared out of the windshield of his brand-new Aston Martin as he put it into park on the sleepy Chiswick street. He'd bought the sports car on impulse two weeks ago, but his James Bond fantasy had hit the skids yesterday, when he'd been forced to spend two hours on paperwork so he could ship it back to the States.

The soft purr of the car's engine was interrupted by the sound of his fingers drumming against the steering wheel. The Aston Martin wasn't his biggest problem at the moment, though.

Why the heck had he agreed to come to Mel's house on Christmas Day?

The way he figured, he'd been suckered into it. She had looked at him with those big doe eyes, told him how much it would mean to her and he'd fallen into the trap without even seeing it.

When he'd dropped her off at her apartment after their meal, the warmth in her eyes, the flush of enthusiasm on her cheeks when she'd insisted he come, had reminded him of the night they'd made love. He had wanted to kiss her in the worse way, but had held back—just to prove that he could.

He hadn't contacted her in the four days since their dinner engagement. He'd wanted to pick up the phone and call her a half-dozen times, but the PR people at Dark Knight were handling the details of the book tour with their customary efficiency so he hadn't been able to come up with a good enough excuse.

He turned off the car's ignition, keeping his eyes on the house in front of him.

Three storeys of terraced Victorian brick stood tall and slightly worn at the end of the dead-end street. He pulled the piece of paper out of his jacket pocket and checked the address written in Mel's neat script. His fingers continued to beat a tattoo against the steering wheel as he looked back up at her parents' home. The lights of a huge Christmas tree twinkled out of the large bay window on the raised first floor of the house. It was only five o'clock, but already darkness engulfed the street. A lone streetlight cast shadows across the small, overgrown front yard, making the brightly coloured lights inside look enchanting.

Jack shook his head, dispelling the romantic notion. What the heck was he doing here? He wasn't into the whole big 'happy family' thing. It wasn't his scene. And he certainly didn't socialise with the families of women he slept with— or was hoping to sleep with. It didn't feel right.

He should turn around right now and drive back to the hotel. He was going to see her on the Eurostar tomorrow anyway— surely he could wait another day? But even as the idea formed in his mind Jack knew he wasn't going to do it. He'd been thinking about seeing her all day. He wanted to see her with that look in her eyes again. Relaxed and happy. The way she'd been at the restaurant when she'd talked about her family.

He took his hands off the steering wheel and rubbed them together. The car was cooling down. Make your mind up, Devlin. Stay or go?

He reached across the seat well, grabbed the spray of flowers and the bottle of pricey Irish malt he'd bought the day before and got out of the car. Slamming the door, he shoved the gifts under one arm, zipped up his leather jacket and sank his hands into the pockets. His boots tapped against the pavement as he mounted the four steps to the front door. The sound of muffled voices and a Motown Christmas song he recognised drifted out into the still night.

He peered in the window, but couldn't see a thing past the tree. His shoulders hunched against the chill as he contemplated the doorbell. And then a memory from one long-ago summer night came flooding back to him.

Peggy Ann Zabriski, that had been her name. Head cheerleader at Mount Jefferson High, two years his senior and the love of his life when he'd been a young and stupid fifteen-year-old. He'd eased himself inside her in her father's old Chevy at Look Out Point. She'd threaded her fingers through his hair and whispered, 'I love you, Jack.' And he'd thought he was the king of the world.

But it was what had come after that made him tense as he stood in the reflected glow of the Christmas tree lights.

Peggy Ann had wanted him to meet her family. She loved him, didn't she? Why didn't he come over one night? Her old man would give him a fair shake. He wouldn't care which side of the tracks Jack came from. Jack hadn't wanted to do it. He'd known what the townspeople thought of him. Thought of what he'd come from. But Peggy Ann had insisted. She couldn't agree to go to the prom with him until he met her folks, could she? So he'd got spruced up, spent his last five dollars on a fancy bunch of flowers and arrived on her doorstep at the allotted time. Her father had opened the door. But as soon as the guy had looked at Jack, his eyes had sharpened with recognition and Jack had known he wasn't going to be taking Peggy Ann to the prom—or anywhere else, for that matter.

Jack shuddered, forced himself to lock the memory away

where it belonged. In that box marked 'another lifetime' where he put all the other memories from his childhood.

What was he so bothered about anyway? It hadn't been that bad—at least he'd never told Peggy Ann he loved her back. When she'd given him the cold shoulder the next day in the school cafeteria, he'd been so grateful for that small fact, he'd promised himself then and there he would never tell any woman he loved her. They were only small, empty words after all; Peggy Ann—and his mother—had shown him that.

Jack stamped his feet against the cold and pressed the doorbell. He wasn't that kid any more. He'd made his life into a staggering success. He could do what he liked, when he liked and if that meant sleeping with Carmel Rourke, then he'd do it—whatever her family might think. But as the shape of someone approaching formed in the frosted-glass panels of the front door Jack's back stiffened.

'My goodness, you must be the writer fellow our Mel's been talking about.' The woman's soft emerald eyes beamed at Jack as she held the door open. 'Well, come on in. You'll be wanting to put your jacket there.' She stepped back into the hallway and gestured towards a row of hooks piled high with coats and scarves. 'Finding a space for it'll be quite a feat, mind you.'

Jack stepped into the welcoming warmth, started to shrug off his jacket, then remembered the hostess gifts under his arm. 'Uh, these are for you,' he said, feeling vaguely ridiculous as he thrust them at her. 'Merry Christmas,' he mumbled.

A wide smile split her face and Jack noticed how pretty she looked and how familiar. She had to be Mel's mother with those high cheekbones, the riot of reddish-brown curls tied back in a fierce bun and the fair, lightly freckled skin—but she didn't look much older than his own thirty-one years.

'That's wonderful, now.' She scooped up the flowers and

liquor and glanced at the label. 'And Jameson's too. Eamon will be singing your praises when we have a drop of this with the pud later.'

'Eileen, woman, where have you hidden the gravy boat?' a shouted voice boomed from the back of the house.

The woman clucked her tongue. 'The man's got two good eyes,' she said in a conspiratorial voice. 'It's a crying shame he's never learned how to use them.' She winked at Jack, then shouted back in her lilting Irish brogue, 'It's right where I left it, of course. Where else would it be?' She patted Jack's arm. 'Come on through. Mel and the rest are in the front room. She'll be all a flutter when she sees you.'

He slung his jacket over the other coats and followed her down the hallway. Paper decorations had been taped to the ceiling and tinsel threaded through the banisters of the main staircase. Shoes and discarded toys were pushed into an alcove and the strong scent of Christmas spices and roasted meat filled the air. Jack noticed a sprig of mistletoe hanging from one of the light fittings and tried not to think about him and Mel standing beneath it.

'I'm Eileen, by the by.' She glanced over her shoulder. 'Mel's mum.'

He nodded, feeling guilty at the direction of his thoughts. 'Devlin, Jack Devlin, ma'am.'

She stopped, pushed a wayward strand of hair away from her face and laughed. 'Goodness, don't ma'am me—you make me feel a hundred years old.'

'You certainly don't look it,' he said without thinking.

'Well, now.' She tilted her head to one side and studied him. 'Handsome as the devil you are and charming with it, Jack Devlin.' The certainty in her voice made him uncomfortable. 'A lethal combination for sure, and I'll be bound you know how to use it.'

Jack didn't know what the hell to say. Her green eyes

seemed friendly, but he was pretty sure the remark hadn't been a compliment.

'Our Mel says you're after taking her off on a trip tomorrow?' she said lightly.

'That's right.' He paused, feeling the urge to justify himself. 'It's a book tour; she's going to be reporting on it.'

'Sounds exciting,' was all she said, but he could have sworn she gave him a shrewd look before opening the door to the living room.

Jack hesitated in the doorway. What exactly had he let himself in for here? He was beginning to think Peggy Ann Zabriski's daddy had nothing on Eileen Rourke.

'Mel, luv, your young man's here.'

Mel sprang off the couch, her eyes lighting on Jack. Her breath caught in her throat. He looked as tall and gorgeous as she remembered him, hovering in the doorway behind her mother.

'Goodness,' Mel heard her sister-in-law Jacie whisper beside her. 'Louisa was right—he's even better-looking in real life.'

Mel felt her cheeks flush as she crossed the living room. The patter of conversations gradually died out and the room fell suspiciously silent. An unheard-of occurrence when the whole of the Rourke clan were in residence.

'Jack,' she said, a little too brightly, her heartbeat hammering in her ears. 'I'm so glad you made it. I thought maybe you'd decided to give it a miss.'

She'd been watching for him all afternoon, ready to jump out of her skin every time the doorbell rang.

He glanced past her to where her family were sitting and she noticed a muscle in his cheek clench. 'I said I'd come,' he said tightly.

Her father gave another plaintive shout from the kitchen.

Mel's mum touched Jack's arm. 'I'll leave you in Mel's capable hands, Jack. I've just got to go hit Mel's father over the head with a gravy boat.'

He nodded. 'Sure, thanks.'

Her mother winked at Mel before heading back out to the kitchen. What was that about?

'I'd better introduce you to everyone.'

He tensed slightly at the suggestion, but nodded again. 'Sure.'

'No introductions necessary,' her brother Christy said from behind her. She'd been so focused on Jack she hadn't even noticed Christy walk over to them with his baby daughter Sofia perched on his hip.

'Christy, Mel's best-looking brother,' he said by way of introduction, and held out his hand.

Jack pulled a hand out of his pocket and shook Christy's. 'Jack Devlin.'

'Nice to meet you, Devlin. Can't believe you're standing in my mum's living room. I've read all your books,' Christy said, bouncing Sofia, who was chewing her fist and staring at Jack as if he had two heads.

The rigid line of Jack's shoulders softened a little. 'Always good to meet a member of the paying public,' he said.

'And there must be a lot of them. You've got a real talent for scaring the life out of people, pal.'

Mel breathed a small sigh of relief. Hearty and handsome, and happily sporting the atrocious Santa Claus jumper their Aunt Maeve had knitted and sent over from Dublin, her brother Christy was a natural-born charmer, as their dad always said. If anyone could get Jack to relax, it was him.

Christy led her and Jack over to everyone else, arranged on the two sofas in front of the tree and busy watching their guest with undisguised interest. Even Mel's three-year-old niece Isabel had stopped banging her new toy set to watch Jack, her eyes almost as wide as her little sister's.

'I'll do the introductions. Seeing as our Mel's lost her tongue,' Christy continued, winking at Mel. 'Not surprising, really, as she's been nattering non-stop about you all afternoon.'

'Oh, yeah?' Jack turned to look at her, the warmth in his gaze making Mel flush.

'N-no, I haven't,' Mel stuttered. Trust Christy to make her feel like a twelve-year-old with her first crush.

'Shut up, Mel, and get our VIP a drink. What you having, Jack?' Christy said, making as if he were Jack's best mate in all the world. 'Our brother Ty's made some fancy-dan American stuff called egg-nog. It's pretty good—loaded with liquor.'

Mel's teeth ground together. Natural-born charmer, indeed. More like natural-born suck-up.

'Sounds great,' Jack said, his eyes still on Mel.

Mel tramped off to the kitchen as Christy began introducing Jack to everyone.

If Christy said one more word to Jack about her, he was going to end up wearing Ty's fancy-dan egg-nog.

'So, I've gotta tell you, Jack, you're a massive improvement on that creep Adam.'

'Who?' Jack's ears perked up at the casual comment from Jamie, who sat on his left and was—if he remembered correctly—the youngest of Mel's older brothers.

Jack had let the family banter wash over him for the last twenty minutes as he'd dug into a plate piled high with turkey, potatoes and a host of crisply roasted vegetables and home-made sauces.

He found it fascinating observing the Rourkes. It had never occurred to him that this was what families were supposed to be like. It had taken over half an hour to get all of them seated at the two tables laid out in the huge open kitchen. During that time, Jack had enjoyed watching Mel deflect the humorous teasing from her big brothers—and give it back as good as she got. He now had a clear idea where that sharp tongue of hers came from, even though it only seemed to come out on special occasions.

The family had asked him a few questions about his work and his latest book, but most of the conversation had been conducted without him, which he'd been grateful for. In fact, what with the delicious food and Mel's knee warm against his under the table, he was feeling more than just grateful.

Mel went still beside him as soon as her brother mentioned this other guy.

'Adam, the prat. That's who,' Jamie continued. 'What a complete—'

'Jamie, be quiet,' Mel interrupted, glaring at her brother. 'Jack's not remotely interested.'

'Actually, he is,' Jack butted in quickly.

'You're not still holding a candle for him, are you?' Jamie's voice was pained, but Jack could hear the concern behind it. 'After what he did.' Now Jack was seriously interested. Who was this jerk?

'No, I'm not,' Mel shot back. 'Now drop it, Jamie.'

'No, don't drop it, Jamie,' Jack said, the spurt of anger surprising him. What had this guy done?

'Don't you dare say another word, Jamie.' Mel's voice rose. She looked at Jack. 'It's none of his business.'

Jack realised he wanted to make it his business. She looked panicked and embarrassed and he wanted to know who had hurt her and how.

'What's going on over there?' All three of them turned. Eamon, Mel's father, was studying them from the head of the table. Everyone else had fallen silent for the first time that evening. Jack tensed, feeling like a five-year-old who'd been caught with his hand in the cookie jar.

'I'll not have you raising your voice to our guest, Carmel.' Eamon gave his daughter a stern look.

'I wasn't shouting at Jack,' Mel replied. 'I was shouting at Jamie.'

Eamon switched his attention to his son. 'And what cause did she have to be shouting at you, James Patrick?'

Jamie gave a long-suffering sigh. 'All I said was that Jack was a big improvement on that creep Adam, and she went into one.'

'I did not,' Mel piped up.

'You did too.'

'Stop.' Eamon held up a meaty palm. 'Now cut it out, both of you, before you give us all indigestion.'

Mel didn't think she'd ever been more mortified in her entire life. Well, okay, maybe Jack finding her in his shower had been worse, but not much. She waited for the heat in her cheeks to subside and tried to force down the last of her turkey.

She could quite happily have strangled Jamie—who'd always been about as subtle as a road accident. But Jack's behaviour was even more unsettling.

Why did he want to know about Adam?

And why did the thought of him finding out the details fill her with horror?

'I think we need to talk about this guy Adam.'

Mel's fork clattered onto her plate at the whispered words. Her head shot round to find Jack studying her. 'No, we don't,' she whispered back. 'It's not important.'

'I think it is,' he said, far too smoothly for her liking.

'So, Jack, you've told us nothing about yourself. What part of America are you from?'

Mel could have kissed her mother as Jack's gaze lifted from hers.

'Pardon, ma'am?' he said, not sounding quite so smooth.

'No need to ma'am me. Eileen will do,' her mother said from the other side of the table. 'I'm after asking where your people are from. Your books never say.'

'I have an apartment in Manhattan,' Jack said, bluntly.

'Manhattan's a lovely place, to be sure. Eamon and I went there for our twentieth wedding anniversary a while back. Is that where your folks are from, then?' her mother said pleasantly, apparently oblivious to the strain in Jack's voice.

Mel knew she ought to intervene and get Jack off the hook. They weren't a couple, so he hardly deserved to be quizzed like this by her mother. But curiosity got the better of her. She'd asked him pretty much the same question herself at The Belvoir and he hadn't given her a proper answer.

'I don't…' Jack paused and swallowed. His eyes ducked to his plate. When he met her mother's enquiring gaze again, his voice sounded flat and remote. 'I don't have any folks.'

A surge of sympathy welled up inside Mel.

'No folks at all?' her mother remarked, clearly as horrified by the thought as Mel. 'But that's terrible, Jack.'

'No, it's not,' he said. 'I don't need them.'

'Of course you do,' her mother said. 'Everybody needs a—'

'Eileen, stop badgering the boy,' her father interrupted, putting his hand over her mother's on the table. 'It's clear he doesn't want to talk about it. Now let it be.'

Her mother looked back at Jack, her eyes shadowed but contrite. 'I should apologise, Jack. I've a bad habit of prying where I shouldn't.'

'No problem.' Jack struggled to keep his voice light. His fist released on the knife he'd been holding in a death grip.

Eamon launched into a lively story about the local football team and Mel's brothers all began to laugh and butt in. Jack breathed out slowly.

'Are you all right?' Mel said softly as her hand covered his on the table.

Her skin felt soft and warm. He turned towards her. Was

that pity he could see in her eyes? Uncomfortable, he pulled his hand away. 'Sure. Why wouldn't I be?'

'No reason,' she said finally, but the concerned look didn't leave her eyes.

'I'm glad you came, Jack.' Mel plastered a smile on her face and tucked her hands into the back pockets of her jeans. 'Now, are you absolutely positive you don't want to stay for charades?'

'I don't think so,' he said, shrugging into the worn leather jacket she remembered seeing in his hotel room. 'After the way Ty aced me at backgammon, I'm quitting while I'm ahead. Your brothers are vicious.'

'You're telling me,' she said, trying to stifle the stab of disappointment.

He zipped up his jacket, bundled his hands into the pockets. 'Say thanks again to your mom and dad. I enjoyed it.'

She wasn't entirely convinced of that. He'd been subdued ever since his conversation with her mother at the dinner table. Mel's own reaction to the knowledge that he had no folks had given her a lot to think about too, but she smiled anyway. 'I will.'

He reached for the door, opened it. The chilled air made her shiver as he stepped outside. She pulled her hands from her pockets and tucked them under her arms.

She was waiting for him to walk down the steps, but he didn't move, just stood with his back to her looking out into the night. Slowly he turned round. He took a step towards her, cupped her elbows in his palms and tugged her outside. Her eyes fixed on his, the hum of awareness almost more than she could bear.

She stood flush against him, but he still hadn't said anything. He wrapped his arms around her and her hands slipped down. The clouds of their breath mingled in the cold air. He felt strong and solid and overwhelming.

'You know what?' His warm breath feathered against her ear. 'There's something I've been wanting to do ever since I saw that mistletoe in your mom's hall.'

'Oh?' She shivered, not sure if the reaction was caused by the cold or the seductive look in his eyes.

'Yeah.' His lips curved against hers. 'You wanna put your hands round my neck, so we can do this properly?'

'Oh, okay.' She reached up and held onto his neck; the hair at his nape felt like silk in her clutching fingers.

He smelt of wine and coffee and leather. The combination was impossibly arousing as his lips covered hers. His tongue teased her and then delved within. The kiss was nothing like the first time. It burned, but with a slow, steady heat, not the hard rush of instant passion. The roughness of his stubble bristled against her cheek. He felt so hot, so hard. His body shuddered as she ran her fingers through his hair.

He lifted his head. 'Merry Christmas, Cinders,' he murmured against her lips.

His hands settled on her waist and he held her still as he stepped back. She let her arms drop to her sides, the sudden chill making her shiver again.

He ran a knuckle down her nose. 'You better get inside before you catch a cold,' he said and smiled. 'I don't want you missing our date at Waterloo tomorrow.'

She watched him walk to his car, gave a heavy sigh. Well, that had given her a whole lot more to think about.

CHAPTER NINE

'YOUR ticket has been upgraded, Mademoiselle Rourke.'

'But that can't be right,' Mel said to the well-groomed young ticket inspector who had come to her rescue. She'd been trying to feed her ticket into the barrier for three minutes, making the businessman behind her huff loudly several times.

'I assure you, this is the case,' the inspector replied in a musical French accent. He brandished a new ticket before feeding it into the terminal. The gates swished open. 'Once you are through Passport Control and Security,' he said, handing the ticket back to her, 'the first-class lounge is at your right. There you have complementary drinks and snacks until you depart.'

Mel dragged her suitcase behind her, clutching her new ticket and feeling even more disorientated. After a virtually sleepless night, she'd spent the last two hours packing and un-packing. What should she wear? Why didn't she have any decent clothes? What exactly would she say to Jack after their kiss on the doorstep the day before? And now this?

How had she ended up with an upgrade? It must be a mistake. Dansworth would never spring for a first-class ticket. Her editor had already given Mel chapter and verse before she left the office for Christmas about her responsibilities to the magazine. 'You're there to get a story, Mel, not have a free holiday, so keep your expenses to an absolute minimum.'

Mel felt guilty enough already about it—knowing the *London Nights* article was about the furthest thing from her mind.

She approached the large double doors to the first-class lounge feeling like an impostor. To her amazement, the uniformed woman at the door let her through without a hitch.

Her eyes found Jack immediately. He was sitting in one of the lounge's plush leather sofas, talking to a tall, expertly groomed young woman. He waved and walked over.

'Hi,' he said. Mel's eyes strayed down to his lips, which were curved in a confidential smile, and flicked back to his face. Don't even go there.

He lifted her suitcase and indicated his companion. 'Come over and meet Alicia. She's our PR contact from Dark Knight.' Figures, thought Mel, ignoring the ridiculous stab of jealousy—only a PR woman could look that good at ten o'clock on Boxing Day morning in Waterloo Station.

'No, wait.' She put a hand on Jack's arm. 'I think there's been a mistake. I shouldn't be here. I've only got an economy-class ticket.'

'No, you haven't. I got you an upgrade.'

'You…' Mel was momentarily struck dumb. 'But the magazine will never agree to that.'

'No sweat. I'm paying for it.'

He put his palm on her back and propelled her across the lounge before she could protest further.

The slim blonde unfolded herself from the sofa and held out a hand to Mel at Jack's introduction. 'It's so nice to meet you, Mel,' she said in the dulcet tones of a woman used to making flattering small talk. 'We couldn't believe it when Jack agreed to have a journalist accompany us. If there's anything you need while we're travelling you must let me know.'

Mel wanted to dislike the woman, but the genuine warmth in her gaze made it impossible. 'Thanks, I will.'

'Jack tells me you're going to be staying at his apartments in Paris and New York.'

'I…' Mel stumbled to a halt as the betraying warmth crept up her neck. 'I think that was the understanding.' What exactly had Jack and Alicia been talking about before she arrived?

'Here, give me your coat,' Jack said, easing the garment off her shoulders. 'I'll go grab you a coffee.' Mel watched him fold the coat over his chair and walk away across the lounge. She perched on the sofa beside Alicia.

Alicia smiled. 'So how long have you and Jack been friends?'

'We're not,' Mel blurted out. 'Not really. We've only met a couple of times.'

Alicia's carefully plucked brows dipped momentarily. 'I'm sorry, I thought…' She hesitated. 'The way Jack talked about you, I thought you were good friends. He guards his privacy so carefully, I assumed he must know you well or he wouldn't trust you—to write the article, I mean.'

'I don't know why he picked me,' Mel said, not quite able to look the PR woman in the eye. 'We're strangers really.' That, at least, was the truth; after all Mel didn't know much more about him than his incredible abilities in bed.

'Hey, now.' She glanced up at the sound of Jack's voice. He put a frothy cup of cappuccino onto the coffee table in front of her. 'I thought we agreed we're not strangers.' He settled in the deep leather armchair opposite, crossing his long legs so that his feet almost touched hers. He looked confident and in control, the glint of amusement in his eye making Mel's cheeks start to burn. For heavens' sake, what exactly had he said to Alicia? Could she possibly look any more unprofessional?

Please don't say anything else, her mind shouted. She stared at him, trying to communicate the message telepathically.

His brow raised in a mocking enquiry. Either he wasn't getting the message, Mel thought irritably, or he was enjoying her discomfort. The smile tugging at his lips made Mel's teeth clench as he turned his attention to Alicia.

'Mel invited me to her family Christmas yesterday. Her folks are great people. I had a lot of fun. Especially when I left,' he added, and winked at Mel. 'Under the mistletoe.'

She never should have kissed him yesterday. Right now, she wanted to pick up the cappuccino and throw it at him. Her face must be the colour of a ripe tomato. Alicia would think she was one of his groupies.

'So you are friends, then,' Alicia said, sounding pleased. 'That's fabulous. Your friendship will add a whole new dimension to the article.'

Wouldn't it just, Mel thought grimly.

'By the way,' Alicia continued eagerly, 'I've spoken to your editor about syndicating the article once it's been published in London. Jack's happy with the idea and we've had approaches from several prestigious titles already.'

Great, Mel thought bitterly. Why don't I write about everything we've done together? Then they can publish the entire thing in *Penthouse*.

'Lighten up, Cinders, or you'll crack a tooth,' Jack whispered in Mel's ear. His hand rested casually on her shoulder as they shuffled up the ramp into the echoing glass and steel structure that covered the Eurostar platform. Alicia, thankfully, was far enough ahead of them in the sea of boarding passengers not to hear their conversation.

Mel's jaw tightened further. 'I'll lighten up if you lay off the Prince Charming routine,' she said, shrugging his hand away. 'Alicia will know we've been...' how should she put it? '...intimate.'

'Yeah, so?' he said equably, settling his hand on the curve of her waist. 'Alicia's a big girl. She won't mind.'

'She might not, but I do. It's a bit unprofessional, don't you think?' Mel turned, dislodging his hand again. 'And I really wish you hadn't upgraded my ticket. It's very generous of you, but it's a bit inappropriate.'

'Inappropriate, huh?' He grinned, those annoying little creases making his eyes look impossibly inviting. 'I don't think so, not after that kiss we shared yesterday.'

'Will you just forget about the kiss?' Even discussing it was making her edgy.

'Sorry, no can do.' His grin spread. 'It's kind of unforgettable.' His eyes flicked down her frame and then came back to her face. 'Like a couple of other things.'

Unfortunately, she was finding it impossible to forget those other things herself. Which would explain why the familiar heat in her stomach was in danger of becoming a raging inferno at the moment and all he was doing was looking at her.

Mel took a step away from him, her suitcase clutched so tightly in her hands she thought she might break a finger. 'Jack, please, could you just back off a bit?' she said wearily.

He bowed his head, gave it a slight shake. When he raised it again, the teasing glint was gone from his eyes. 'Okay, fine.' He skimmed a finger down her cheek. 'We'll play it your way for a while, Cinders. But I'm not going to forget about that kiss—or the rest of it.'

'All right,' she said, knowing she wasn't going to be forgetting anything either.

'Let's get aboard.' He took her case, stood back so she could mount the stairs of their carriage. 'We don't want Alicia getting the wrong idea,' he said, dryly.

He stowed his holdall and her suitcase at the end of the aisle, then they walked down the carriage together. His hand rested on her waist. Mel welcomed the weight of it, unable to deny herself the small intimacy any longer—whatever Alicia might think.

'And just for the record, Cinders,' he murmured against her

neck as they approached their seats, 'I didn't get you an upgrade to be generous.'

It wasn't until the powerful Eurostar train was bulleting through South London, Mel rocking gently in her seat as Jack chatted to Alicia about the book signings, that she accepted the truth. Just seeing him again, talking to him again, was like an aphrodisiac. And she thought she would be able to keep her hands off him until she got to know him better. It finally dawned on her that she didn't have a hope in hell of pulling it off.

They arrived in Paris in the early afternoon. The heaving disarray of the commuter platform at Gare du Nord was a far cry from the sleek exclusivity of the Waterloo terminal. Alicia waved them goodbye at the taxi rank, giving Mel a brief hug and pressing her card into her hand. Whatever Mel's tumultuous thoughts during the two-and-a-half-hour journey, she couldn't deny she liked Alicia, a lot. The PR woman was supremely efficient but also genuinely friendly—and her being there had helped to divert Mel's thoughts from her other travelling companion and the rising panic about what exactly she was going to do when she was alone with him.

As soon as Alicia was gone, Mel expected Jack to turn up the charm again. Even knowing that he was only after one thing, Mel knew she wouldn't be able to resist him much longer. How exactly did you go about resisting the irresistible? And anyway, she was becoming pretty sure she didn't want to.

But, to her surprise, he kept his distance. There were no more mentions of 'that kiss' or 'that night' during the cab ride to the Place des Vosges. He was friendly, but aloof, asking her about how well she knew Paris, explaining how he'd lived there for a year after publishing his first novel. After he rattled off their destination to the cabbie in French, Mel felt a little ashamed that he, 'an American', spoke the language like a native, while she, who lived in a neighbouring country, could barely order a croissant without making a fool of herself.

His apartment on the stately, much-sought-after square in the heart of the Marais turned out to be almost as irresistible as the man himself. She found herself holding her breath as he gave her a brief tour. The high ceilings, large, lushly furnished rooms, and ornate glass-panelled doors that led out onto the wrought-iron balconies overlooking the stately gardens below suggested a palatial elegance that she'd only ever seen before in the pages of magazines.

He left her in one of the guest bedrooms, explaining he had to make a few calls. Mel listened to his footsteps retreat down the hallway, sighed and flopped on the bed. The feathered duvet and quilt, springy mattress and exquisitely carved headboard made her feel like a fairy-tale princess. She turned her head. The winter sun hung low in the sky outside, shining through the floor-to-ceiling French doors that looked onto the square. Pushing herself upright, she climbed down from the bed and went over to the glass. She'd have liked to open the doors and step out onto the iron balcony, but the room was wonderfully warm, heat pumping out of the old-fashioned radiators, and she didn't want to bring in the chill.

Through the bare trees that edged the square, she could see a young couple snuggled together on one of the park's benches. The man's arm placed casually around the woman's shoulder, he hugged her to him as they chatted. Mel sighed again, feeling an odd lump of anticipation and regret lodge in her throat.

The romance of this city, this beautiful place, was already weaving its spell on her. She might as well stop pretending now. She was a goner.

Jack watched her from the doorway of the room, saw the heavy sigh and felt like even more of a low-life. Even knowing that, he had to force himself not to march across the room and take her in his arms. He wanted her in the worst way. The desire hadn't lessened one bit since their night together at The Ritz. Something about her captivated him, that odd combination of confidence and uncertainty. Her profile looked so delicate lit by the dying sun, the deep chestnut highlights in her hair making her skin look almost translucent.

She'd practically begged him to stop pressuring her at the station and he'd had to force himself to take a step back. He'd seen the wariness in her eyes, heard the weariness in her voice. He had to slow down, give her space.

She'd kissed him back so passionately yesterday, he knew she didn't really want to resist him any more. But why did his patience, his practised charm, seem to have deserted him so completely with this woman? The teasing, the flirting he usually enjoyed as a precursor to lovemaking had become a double-edged sword with her. Sure, he loved flirting with her, loved the way she got all feisty and animated when he sparked her off. But afterwards, it was harder than it had ever been for him not to take what he wanted.

She sighed again and turned. She tensed when she spotted him in the doorway, her cheeks colouring.

He leaned against the doorjamb. 'Madame Marinez, the housekeeper, left us some logs. I thought I'd build a fire and then we could go grab some supper at the little restaurant round the corner,' he said as calmly as he could.

'All right.' She glanced at her watch. 'But it's only four o'clock—are you hungry already?'

I'm starving, he thought, but didn't say it. He wasn't thinking about food.

'We could go for a walk first, if you like.' No way was he staying in the apartment alone with her any longer than was absolutely necessary. He wasn't a damn saint, after all.

'Great.' She didn't sound all that enthusiastic. 'I'll unpack my stuff. I'll be out in a minute.'

Jack strode back into the living room and began dumping the logs into the fireplace. He had no doubt at all he wasn't going to get a wink of sleep tonight.

The tiny little bistro round the corner from Jack's flat lacked the ornate splendour of The Belvoir but seemed even more romantic to Mel. The crammed tables were peopled entirely by couples, all talking in animated French. The fog of cigarette smoke, cooked garlic and warm bodies added to the air of intimacy.

Jack translated the menu, which was written on a blackboard over the bar, and then ordered for them both. A few minutes later, the waiter dumped a carafe of red wine, a basket of French bread and two hearty bowls of bouillabaisse onto the table with a distinct lack of pomp and circumstance.

'So, why don't you tell me about this Adam guy?' Jack asked, picking up his spoon.

Mel paused, her spoon halfway to her mouth; the personal question had come as a bit of a shock. During their walk through the Marais, Jack had kept the conversation light and impersonal and had been careful not to touch her. She should have been glad, but actually it had made her feel needy. Still, she didn't want to talk about Adam. That was a bit too personal.

'There's nothing much to tell,' she said, keeping her tone bland, and bent her head to sip the spicy broth. The silence stretched out between them. She huffed out a breath. He was watching her, waiting for her to continue. 'We met at this bar near the magazine. We hit it off, went out for a while. Then, one day, the wife I didn't know he had turned up at my flat. End of story.'

So that explains it, Jack thought, seeing the hurt and humiliation in her gaze before it slid back to her bowl. 'Your brother was right, then, the guy was a jerk.'

'Yes, he was,' she said softly, still concentrating on her food.

The urge to comfort her came from nowhere. Jack laid his hand over hers. He felt her tremble as her eyes lifted. 'How long were you dating?'

'Nearly three months.' She gave a half-laugh, shrugged. 'Pathetic, isn't it? That I managed to miss the obvious for so long.' She took her hand out from under his, looked down at her lap. 'I mean, he never came round at weekends. In fact, we didn't go out much at all. Mostly, we just had sex, but I never suspected a thing.'

Jack felt a strange pressure in his chest. Was that why she'd panicked after their night at The Ritz? Because it had been just sex? 'Did you love him?'

Mel glanced up. His brows were drawn together, his eyes hooded. He looked serious.

She sighed, shook her head. 'No, I didn't love him.' Was that relief she saw flash in his eyes? 'But I trusted him.' She paused. Talking about it wasn't as hard as she'd thought it would be. 'We had fun together. I really liked him. I thought I was his friend.' She swallowed down the shame. 'When, actually, I was just his bit on the side. And, according to his wife, I wasn't the first either.'

'Is that what spooked you?'

'What?' Mel asked, confused by the statement.

'At The Ritz. Did you think I might be married?'

She glanced back at her bowl, surprised he had been so perceptive. 'Yes, it did occur to me the morning after.' She looked up. 'It took me a long time to get over my encounter with Adam's wife. For months I kept remembering how angry and upset she'd been.' Her eyes fixed on the paper tablecloth, seeing the woman's tear-soaked face. 'I'd hurt her so badly. I couldn't bear to do that to another woman.'

He tucked a knuckle under her chin, lifted her face. 'Mel,

you didn't hurt her, he did. Some guys get a kick out of cheating. Adam was one of those guys.' He stroked her cheek with his thumb and dropped his hand. 'If he hadn't done it with you, he would have done it with someone else.'

She gave a weak smile, taking another mouthful of soup. Funny, but his simple analysis was more comforting than all the words of consolation she'd got from Louisa and her other friends at the time. 'You sound like an expert,' she said.

His eyebrow winged up as he swallowed. 'On cheating?'

'No.' She laughed, he looked so affronted. 'On marriage.'

He pushed the empty bowl away, a wry grin tugging at his lips. 'Not exactly. That's one subject I don't know a thing about.'

And from the look on his face, she suspected he didn't want to.

'But I'll tell you what.' He leaned forward, propping his elbows on the table. 'When I'm dating a woman, I don't cheat on her. Once things have run their course, I tell her.'

'Are you always the one who does the telling, Jack?'

He shrugged. 'Not always,' he said, looking away to signal the waiter.

The waiter took their bowls, then reeled off the dessert menu.

'How does mousse *au chocolat* sound?' Jack asked. Mel nodded and he ordered.

She waited until the waiter had left and Jack had finally turned his attention back to her. 'But nine times out of ten, it's you who ends it,' she said.

Suspicion clouded his eyes. 'What are you getting at?'

Why not just ask him? She already knew the answer. 'How many long-term relationships have you had, Jack?'

His eyes widened and he shifted in his chair. The waiter put their dessert plates on the table. *'Merci,'* Jack said absently. 'Tuck in.' He gestured with the spoon and scooped up a huge section of his mousse. 'It's good, I guarantee it.'

She savoured the dark chocolaty taste on her tongue and

waited. She watched him scrape the small ramekin clean. Still he didn't say anything. She took another mouthful. Silence.

'You didn't answer my question, Jack.'

His spoon clattered into the empty bowl. 'Look, Cinders, I'll level with you.' His voice sounded strained. 'I'm not a long-term kind of guy.'

Jack tried to gauge her reaction. His palms were sweating and the chocolate mousse he'd stuffed down tasted like tar. What was bothering him? He was only telling her the truth.

He always made it plain right from the start of any relationship what he was looking for. Fun, good sex, friendship, maybe—but only in the short-term.

He never lied about his intentions. What would be the point? It would only make things messy later on. But he'd considered lying to her. Knowing what that jerk Adam had done to her, he knew he couldn't, but for a moment he'd wanted to.

She didn't look devastated by his admission. In fact, she didn't even look surprised. His palms, though, were still damp.

He rubbed them on his jeans. 'I think we've got a lot of chemistry,' he said.

'Sexual chemistry, you mean.'

That stopped him. Okay, she was being direct. That was good, wasn't it? That was what he wanted. 'Yeah, I guess.'

The waiter took their dessert plates and placed the tab on the table. Jack shifted forward in his seat and took her hand, suddenly desperate to touch her. 'We've got a couple of weeks together. Let's see where it goes? It could be a lot of fun?'

Yes, Mel thought, the feel of his thumb caressing the back of her hand doing strange things to her insides. Yes, it could be fun. She'd had the best sex of her life in that hotel room and even now she yearned for his touch.

Maybe she should stop worrying about tomorrow and start

thinking about what she had today. He'd been honest with her, and surprisingly sympathetic as well.

Maybe it was time she stopped trying to be a nun. If no-strings sex was all he offered, maybe that was enough. In fact, maybe it was exactly what she needed right now. After all, she was hardly looking for the long-term herself.

But still she hesitated. 'Could I say I'd like to think about it?'

'Sure, no pressure, I promise.' He raised his hands, grinned at her, looking both relieved and pleased. 'Why don't we drink to that?' he said, pouring more wine into their glasses. 'Listen, the book signing's been scheduled for tomorrow at Galeries Lafayette,' he said, taking some Euros out of his pocket and throwing them on the table. 'I've got meetings beforehand with the French publisher and then the translator on the new manuscript. You want to come along?'

'I think I might do some sightseeing.' She needed a bit of time alone, even if it was only to get used to the idea. 'But I'll need to meet you there if you let me know the time.'

As they strolled back across the Place des Vosges, their feet crunching on the gravel pathway, she realised she was looking forward to the rest of the trip. His hand rested casually on her waist. He was right, they could have a lot of fun—they'd certainly had fun before. Excitement leapt in her belly. Okay, so neither of them was looking for anything serious, but it would still be fascinating to get to know him better while they were having their fun. What harm could it do?

He gave her a chaste kiss on the forehead before they went to their separate bedrooms. It was enough to keep Mel tossing and turning most of the night.

CHAPTER TEN

'WE'RE out of here.' Jack gripped Mel's hand and pulled her past the forty-foot Christmas tree that filled the magnificent domed atrium of Galeries Lafayette.

She heard a shout behind her as Jack held the heavy glass door open and dragged her out into the night. Snow sprinkled down, dampening the pavements and making people pull their collars up and wrap their coats tight as they rushed past on Boulevard Haussmann.

She glanced over her shoulder to see Eli and his PR people following them out through the grand store's palatial entrance lobby. 'Eli's signalling you,' she said as she buttoned her coat.

Jack wrapped his arm around her. 'He can catch me later,' he murmured without looking round. He raised two fingers to his lips. The piercing whistle made Mel jump.

A cab screeched to the kerb. Jack opened the door and bundled her into the dark, musty interior.

'*Au Père Lachaise, s'il-vous plaît,*' he shouted into the driver's grill.

Mel looked past him to the department store's entrance. Eli ran out onto the kerb just as the cab sped off into the sea of traffic along the wide, tree-lined street.

'I think Eli had something to say to you.'

Jack settled back, put his arm across the seat behind Mel's head and eased out a breath. 'He'll get over it.' He rested his hand casually on the side of her neck, brushed his thumb across the sensitive skin. 'He's had his pound of flesh for today.'

Mel shifted slightly; his thumb was doing disturbing things to her pulse-rate. 'You hate it, don't you?'

He brought his arm back down. 'Hate what?'

'All the attention.'

He shrugged, rubbed his hands together before looking back at her. 'I figured I did a pretty good job in there.'

'Oh, you did.' She touched his knee, felt the solid warmth beneath her palm. 'That's not what I meant at all. You were fantastic.'

She'd watched him for nearly three hours, scribbling his autograph and an array of personalised messages into his books, talking in flawless French to the fans who had queued round the block in the frigid wind to meet him. He'd insisted on seeing and talking to every one of them. That was why the signing had lasted twice as long as its allotted time.

'But you didn't enjoy it,' she murmured. 'And you refused to answer any of the reporters' questions.'

'It wasn't supposed to be a press conference. I was there to meet the people who buy and read my books, not the damn press.'

It had been almost comical, she thought, how he'd ignored the shouted questions from the reporters thronged around the signing table and concentrated solely on the public.

The cab hit a bump, jostling them both and making Mel's shoulder thud against the door.

'Come here.' Jack pulled her across the seat. 'It's safer.' He settled his arm around her shoulders. 'That's better,' he said. She could feel his breath ruffling her hair. It felt so good to be held at last, she thought. He was warm and solid beside her. The smell of him male and inviting.

It seemed as if he'd been touching her all day long. All through the signing he'd insisted she stay by his side. She was so aware of him. Every time he so much as looked at her now, she felt as if she were going to melt into a puddle at his feet.

The cab veered round a sharp bend and Jack's arm tightened around her. Mel looked out of the window. The hectic traffic snarl of the Place de la Bastille looked almost picturesque through the snow flurries.

'Where are we going?' she asked warily. If they were headed back to the apartment, she was in big trouble.

'I've got somewhere I want to show you.'

She should have been relieved, but she wasn't. Okay, she was in very big trouble.

The cab came out from a side street, the cramped lines of terraced apartment buildings giving way to a cobble-stoned hill with what looked like a park spread out before them.

'We're here,' Jack said, then leaned forward and tapped the driver's grill. *'Vous pouvez nous déposer ici. C'est bien.'*

He paid the cabbie as Mel stepped out onto the street. Cast-iron railings stretched into the distance up the hill. The street-lamps cast a foggy glow through the bare trees and light dusting of snow. Squinting into the shadows, Mel could see a row of monuments in the park.

'What is this place?'

'Père Lachaise—most romantic place in Paris,' Jack replied, putting his arm round Mel's shoulder and steering her towards a pair of forbidding iron gates with a large padlock chained across them.

She peered into the grounds. 'It's a graveyard,' she said in astonishment.

'Yup,' he replied.

'And it's locked.'

'It's packed with tourists during the day. The atmosphere's much better at night.'

'But, how will we—'

'I'll give you a boost.' He turned her to face him, bent down and threaded his fingers together in a sling.

She stared down at them. 'I can't...'

'Don't be chicken.' A challenging smile tugged at his lips as his eyes met hers. 'You know, I expected more guts from a girl who'd break into a stranger's hotel room in the middle of the night.'

'I didn't break in, I—' she began, then saw his smile spread. 'Oh, for goodness' sake.'

He lifted her up easily and followed her, levering himself over in one quick, graceful movement and then helping her down from the top.

She shivered, staring at the row of elaborate tombstones and statues, dedicated to the dead. 'It's eerie.'

'No, it's not.' He took her hand, swung it gently as he led her into the shadows. 'It's beautiful.'

Their footsteps echoed on the stone pathway as they passed the row of graves.

'Piaf, Balzac, Wilde—everyone who's anyone and died in Paris is buried here,' Jack said. 'Even Jim Morrison, the poor guy. Some of the monuments on the graves are incredible. Look over there.'

He pointed to a white stone sculpture, given an unearthly glow by the full moon that shone through the trees. A young woman in the first flush of motherhood nursed a smiling baby at her naked breast.

Mel caught her breath. 'She looks so real. And so happy.'

'See, I told you. It's not creepy. It's life-affirming—in a weird kind of way.'

'Who was she?'

He squatted down, still holding Mel's hand. '"Segolene Antoinette LaGrande."' He read out. '"Née en 1850, décédée en 1882."' He cursed quietly. 'She was only thirty-two. It says she had…' he whistled '…wow, six kids.' He stood up. 'Guess that explains the tombstone.'

'That's so sad,' Mel whispered.

'Not really, at least she made the most of the time she had.' He draped his arm over her shoulder. 'The best one's down here. But keep your voice down.'

'Why?'

'This place has a twenty-four-hour guard thanks to good ole Jim and his fans.'

Mel stopped dead on the path. 'You mean we could get caught?' she whispered furiously.

He just grinned and pulled her back to his side. 'Don't panic. This is France. Once they see we're lovers on a tryst, they won't arrest us.'

'But we're not,' she whispered back.

'Says who?'

She felt the giddy leap of her heart at his words. Okay, she was in very, very big trouble.

They continued to walk in silence, until he stopped in front of a magnificent grey stone monument, an elaborate etching of a girl and a man entwined on the front. 'Here it is. Abelard and Heloïse.'

'Who were they?'

'Legendary French lovers. He was a philosopher. She was his student. They fell in love, ran away together. You name it, their story's got it. Illegitimate kid, wicked uncle, secret marriage, heartache, self-sacrifice, undying love, the works.'

'What happened to them in the end?'

He turned, rested his hands on her hips. He was so close she could smell him, the lovely intoxicating scent that was uniquely his.

'Like all great tragedies, it gets kind of gruesome at the end,' he murmured. Reaching up, he pushed a curl of hair behind her ear. 'The deal is—' his eyes fixed on her face

'—if you're looking for true love, you come to their tomb and leave a note.'

Her heart banged against her chest. The snow had stopped, but he still had a few tantalising crystals of ice on his dark, wavy hair.

'So what are *we* doing here?' she said, breathlessly.

He skimmed a finger down her cheek. 'I don't know about you...' he cupped her cheeks in cold palms, angled her face up to his '...but I'm admiring the view.'

He nipped at her bottom lip. Her breath caught in her throat.

'Jack.' The word gushed out on an unsteady sigh. 'You're not seriously planning to seduce me in a graveyard, are you?'

'Sure I am.' He murmured the words against her cheek. She could feel the curve of his lips. The skin of her nape tingled as his fingers caressed. 'I'm a crime novelist. Cemeteries are my forte.'

She shuddered as his lips worked their way around her neck and he licked the pulse point. She dragged trembling hands up, placed them firmly against his jacket. She eased him back.

'Jack, we're surrounded by dead people.' It was the only objection she could think of.

He laughed, the sound low and rough. 'But you're forgetting, honey. These are dead French people. They won't mind a bit.'

His lips covered hers then, all teasing gone as his tongue demanded entry. She gripped the back of his neck, her gloved fingers clumsy.

They came together in a whirlwind of need, a sudden inferno of heat and longing. The strong surge of arousal shocked her. He pressed her back against the stone, his lips devouring her mouth as he grasped her hips and lifted her up. His leg pushed against hers, until her core rubbed hard against his thigh through the thick layers of clothing. The heat surged through her, making her ache.

He lifted his head, his ragged pants matching her own.

'Damn it, I want you naked,' he groaned.

She laughed, desire and euphoria making her light-headed. 'There's no way I'm stripping off in a graveyard in the middle of winter. I don't care how French it is.'

'Fair enough.' He chuckled. 'Just for the record, though, is it the dead people, the cold or the getting naked you object to?'

She giggled, feeling reckless. Who was she kidding? She wanted him as much as he wanted her. 'That would be yes to the first and the second, no to the third.'

He cocked his head, frowned. 'Is that no you object or no you don't object to the—'

'For goodness' sake.' She huffed. 'Shut up, Jack, and let's get back to your flat, so we can both get naked before I explode.'

It took an eternity to get back. They stayed apart in the cab, Jack's hand squeezing hers as they bumped through the streets in silence. The regrets, the worries, the fears Mel might have expected during that interminable ride didn't come, though.

She didn't care any more about consequences or responsibilities or where this was all leading. All she could think about was the feel of his lips, rough and urgent on hers. His hands fisted in her hair. The memory of him deep inside her from that magical night at The Ritz.

She'd held out against his industrial-strength charm for long enough—which was probably a record for any woman. But what had she been trying to prove? Looking at his handsome profile in the dim light of the cab, knowing he was hers, even if it was only for tonight, intoxicated her. She felt beautiful, irresistible and so full of pure, animal lust she wanted to scream.

'That's gotta be the longest cab ride of my life,' Jack growled as he kicked the door closed to the apartment and thrust Mel up against the wall.

He tore open the buttons of her coat and pushed it off her

shoulders. Then his lips found hers. The kiss was firm and demanding but fleeting. She moaned as he drew back. Pulling off his jacket, he threw it to the floor. His hands gripped her waist. She gasped as his cold fingers trailed up under her camisole and the several layers of cotton and wool above it. She struggled to get her gloves off as his hands stroked up her back, finding the hook of her bra. He fumbled, then cursed loudly.

'How many layers have you got here?'

She kissed his jaw, felt him shudder as she threaded her fingers through the hair at his nape. 'You're not giving up already, are you?'

'What do you think?' he said, grinning back at her.

She helped as best she could as he pulled the layers off. Her cardigan, her sweater, her cotton T-shirt and camisole all hit the floor in a matter of seconds. The bra followed moments later. She felt the blush hit her cheeks as he stared down at her.

'God, you're beautiful,' he murmured. He cupped her breast, grazed a thumb across her nipple. He watched as the tip hardened and then stroked the underside. She gasped, already throbbing with need. His eyes fixed on her face and then he pressed her back, his teeth tugged on her lower lip. She writhed, feeling the arrow of heat plunge down to her core as his fingers sank into her hair and his lips fastened on hers.

Reaching with trembling hands, she tugged up his thin black jumper. The feel of the firm, velvet flesh beneath made her shiver. He shuddered, eased back and pulled his jumper over his head.

The hard wall of his chest flattened her breasts as he kissed her again, hard and deep. One hand cradled her head, while the other reached down. His thumb brushed the side of her breast, then she heard the rasp of her zipper. Strong fingers delved into the slick, swollen folds of her sex and rubbed at the heart of her.

She jerked away from his lips, choking out a sob. 'Don't,' she moaned. 'I'll come.'

'Honey, that's the idea.' His voice sounded rough as he continued to stroke the swollen nub, ruthlessly stoking the flames as she bucked under his hand and clung to his shoulders. She cried out, her body shattering as she soared to peak.

Jack eased his hand out of her pants. The way she responded to him was incredible. He'd never seen anything more beautiful than the way she'd just fallen apart in his arms. He had to have the biggest hard-on of his life—and he wanted to bury it inside her so badly it hurt. In fact, it was kind of scary how badly he wanted her. He wasn't going to worry about that now. He slung an arm under her knees and lifted her limp body against his chest. His heart jolted when she put her arms round his neck and held on.

'Don't you dare fall asleep. We're not through yet.'

Mel couldn't have fallen asleep now if she'd taken a lorryload of sleeping pills. She felt as if she were drifting on a sea of sensation. The beat of his pulse, the heat of his skin, the tingle of his chest hair against her breast. Every feeling was magnified a hundred times.

She held on tight to his neck, sighed when he placed her down on the bed. The urgency was gone, for her at least. But when he pulled her trousers and socks off in one move and then followed with his own, she realised the same wasn't true for him. His erection jutted out as he knelt beside her. She felt the heady rush of desire return as she looked at it, the heat building at her core. She reached out and ran the tip of her finger down the length of him.

His flesh leapt at the small touch and he shifted away. 'Don't, or I'll explode,' he said, his voice strained.

She looked up. 'But, honey,' she said coquettishly, 'I thought that was the idea.' She giggled as his brows drew together.

'Okay, you asked for it.'

The sensual threat made her shiver as she watched him grab a condom out of the bedside table. Grasping her hips, he dragged her across the bed, until she was under him. The yearning inside her reached fever pitch as he probed gently and then eased within. His entry was difficult, her swollen sex adjusting slowly to his size. His shaft was so hard and so full inside her the stretched feeling was almost unbearable. The pulse of pleasure at her core was so raw, she heard herself moan.

'God, that feels fantastic,' he groaned.

Then he started to move, slowly at first, pushing deeper, taking more, until she was sure she would shatter again. But each time he withdrew just short of completion. Then the strokes increased faster, and harder, forcing her closer to the edge. Her body bucked, the swell of ecstasy building to breaking-point. She screamed as the wave of pleasure broke over inside her and heard him shout out above her.

He collapsed on top of her, pushing her deep into the mattress. She could hear his ragged breathing, could still feel him pulsing inside her. The weight of him felt good, felt right somehow. She lifted limp hands and ran them up the damp skin of his back.

'Am I crushing you?' he muttered beside her head.

'I don't know. I've gone numb.'

He laughed, levered himself up. He smiled as he looked down at her. 'You know, I've gotta say, I'm not a patient guy, but that was definitely worth the wait, Cinders.'

Mel had to agree with him. 'And you know what we've got to do now, don't you, Prince Charming?' she said.

'What?' he asked, holding her hips, his sex still firm inside her.

'Make up for lost time.'

His eyes gleamed and his smile turned into a wicked grin. 'You got that right.'

CHAPTER ELEVEN

FORGET Paris in the springtime, Mel decided over the following days. Paris in the middle of winter was the perfect time for lovers.

Jack knew the city well, and seemed eager to show her all it had to offer. They had two days before they had to catch the plane to New York and, with the book signing already out the way, Paris was theirs for the taking.

After a late start their second morning—a very, very late start—Jack hauled her over to the back streets of the Latin Quarter where they took in an old black-and-white movie in one of the area's tiny picture houses. Mel didn't understand a word, the film being a sixties French classic about a street thief and a beautiful young American girl. But with Jack whispering the pertinent bits to her in English, his breath making her earlobe tingle and his arm slung casually around her shoulder, it didn't take her long to get the gist of it. They got so turned on, they ended up in the back row necking like a couple of teenagers until the grumpy old fellow in the row ahead shouted the French equivalent of 'get a room' at them. Jack dutifully translated the remark for her, before they took the guy up on his suggestion.

They gawked at the modern structural splendour of the Pompidou Centre, walked arm in arm along the Seine in the rain and fed themselves to a standstill at all Jack's favourite restaurants and cafés, Jack insisting he had to have three main meals a day no matter what. They visited his 'favourite of favourites', a traditional Parisian brasserie tucked away in an alley behind the Bastille. Mel felt as if she'd stepped back in time to the days of Toulouse Lautrec when she walked through the restaurant's revolving door: the white tablecloths, oak floors and brass fittings perfectly matching the smoke-stained wallpaper and wait staff who brandished platters of seafood and sauerkraut in long white aprons and crisp black waistcoats.

While Jack spent Wednesday afternoon in a meeting with his French agent, Mel began working on the article. The words flowed easily. Concerns about her unprofessionalism were pushed aside as she made the decision to write a strong, informative piece about Jack's literary achievements rather than his private life. It might not be what Dansworth was expecting, but it was what she was going to get, Mel decided.

Although Mel wasn't getting a huge amount of sleep, she felt energised, riding on a crest of adrenaline and arousal. Living in the moment wasn't just fun, it was fantastic. And in just a few short days she'd come to know some intriguing things about her lover. Other than just his voracious appetite for her, he loved old soul music, oysters in their shell and black-and-white movies. He hated jazz and mobile phones and he never seemed to be full, no matter how much he ate. By Wednesday evening, though, Mel was sure she couldn't take another three-course culinary experience without exploding.

'I know a little North African place not far from here that does great couscous. How about we head there for supper?'

'Hmm?' Mel stretched, her blood still fizzing from another amazing orgasm.

Jack leaned over her, gripped her chin and placed a quick kiss on her lips. 'Stop tempting me, woman,' he said, and gave her bare bottom a pat. 'Out of bed, before I get other ideas and we both end up starving to death.'

'There's absolutely no chance of you starving to death,' Mel said dreamily as he got out of the bed. 'I've never seen anyone eat like you do.'

Goodness, the man was gorgeous, she thought as she watched him stroll over to the chest of drawers, gloriously naked. Broad, well-muscled shoulders, a lean waist and—she tilted her head to one side as he slipped on his boxer shorts— that had to be the best butt this side of Brad Pitt. Actually, forget Brad Pitt, Jack's could beat Brad's hands down. And then there were his pecs, she thought as he turned to fish a clean T-shirt out of the top drawer. Mel's mouth watered—and then her stomach grumbled.

Jack laughed. 'You see, I'm not the only one needs feeding.' He pushed a thick lock of hair off his forehead and pulled on his T-shirt.

Sitting up, Mel lifted the sheet up to cover her breasts and watched as he got the rest of his clothes on. There was something so wonderfully intimate about knowing how a man got dressed.

'I know, let's stay in this evening,' she said.

Jack looked up as he fastened his jeans. 'I guess we could get take-out.'

'Why don't we cook?' Mel scooted over to the side of the bed still wrapped in the sheet. 'There's a lovely little market next to the metro station. We could pick some food up, rustle something simple up.' She let the sheet drop and bent to pick up her knickers.

She heard his footsteps behind her as she put them on. Warm hands caressed her belly from behind, making her shiver. He pulled her back against his chest, nuzzled her ear. 'That's so cute,' he murmured. 'You want to cook for me.'

Mel turned in his arms and fastened her lips onto his. She

ran her fingers through his hair, pulled him closer still and ravished his mouth. She didn't think she'd ever get enough of that mouth. She stepped back, and smiled sweetly. 'I didn't say I'd cook. I said we'd cook. I'm not *that* cute.'

He reached out to tug her back into his arms, but she danced away. 'Uh-uh.' She wagged her finger at him. 'There's no time for that—you're starving, remember? And the market will probably be closed pretty soon. It's getting dark outside.'

'Right.' He stepped forward, frowning slightly. 'All the more reason to eat out, then.'

'Jack,' Mel said, sighing. 'We've been eating out three times a day everyday so far. It'll be nice to stay in for a change.'

She could picture a cosy evening by the fire. Crusty French bread, a fluffy omelette, some green beans maybe, a nice Chablis—and the possibility of something carnal for dessert.

She fastened her bra, put on her own jeans. He continued to frown at her. 'What's wrong?' she asked as she buttoned up her shirt.

His eyes followed the course of her fingers. He looked up once the last button was fastened. 'Look, the truth is I don't cook much. I don't even think there's anything here to cook with.'

'You're kidding?'

He just raised an eyebrow.

'Let's go and have a look,' she said.

Five minutes later, Mel had searched the kitchen cabinets and found one battered milk saucepan, a few small side plates, an odd assortment of cutlery and a sachet of sugar.

'I don't believe it. You're in the culinary capital of the world and you don't even have a frying-pan.'

'Don't look at me like that,' he said, disgruntled. 'Why would I cook if I can eat out?'

Mel looked into his exasperated face. Her eyes narrowed. 'Wait a minute. Have you ever cooked? Do you even know how?'

'Big deal,' he said, not remotely ashamed. 'Why should I know how to cook?'

'Because you eat, you bozo. In fact, you eat a lot.'

'So, I'm a guy and I'm loaded. I eat out.'

No wonder he'd insisted they go out for breakfast every morning. Did he even know how to brew a pot of coffee? 'Do you have any idea how totally lame that sounds, Jack? In case you haven't noticed we live in the twenty-first century.' She strode into the living room and grabbed her purse. 'I've got news for you, buddy. Real men don't only eat quiche these days, they know how to cook it too.'

'Quiche? You mean flan. I hate flan.'

'Yes, well, that's good, because flan's probably way beyond your capabilities, actually.' She took his jacket off the back of the sofa, threw it at him. He caught it one-handed. 'We'll start with an omelette,' she said. 'Simple and delicious. Perfect, seeing as we're obviously going to be starting from scratch here.'

'But what about the frying-pan? We don't have one, remember?' He sounded just a little bit desperate.

She walked back to him, patted his cheek. 'You're going to go downstairs and ask Madame Marinez if we can borrow one.' She took her bag off her arm, dug around until she found a pen and a piece of scrap paper. 'I'll make you a list of the things we'll need.'

'I'm not going to go beg cookware off my housekeeper.' He looked horrified. 'If you're so all-fired desperate to cook supper, you should do it.'

'With my French we'd probably end up with a hair-dryer and a toilet brush. Don't worry, Jack.' She grinned. He was cute when he was flustered. 'She won't think you're less of a man because you want to borrow some cooking utensils.'

'How the hell do you know?'

He continued to grumble as they walked down the stairs to Madame Marinez's apartment. 'The way I see it, a real man's someone who can give you multiple orgasms. Not someone who can rustle up a three-course meal,' he muttered.

Mel shook her head as they stopped in front of the Marinez apartment. 'Haven't you ever heard the phrase, "you can't live on great sex alone"?' she said jauntily.

'No, I haven't.'

She laughed as she pressed the doorbell.

'Okay, now you need to put in a knob of butter.'

'A what?'

'Here you go.' Mel reached across him and dropped the butter into the hot frying pan.

Jack watched it sizzle, and wondered for about the twenty-fifth time in the last half an hour how he'd ended up with a dishtowel tucked into his jeans doing domestic chores.

The humiliating experience of asking Madame Marinez for Mel's list of cookware—none of which he knew the names for in French, despite being as good as fluent in the language—had been bad enough. But when the old woman had treated him to a ten-minute lecture on the importance of having your own cookware, he'd been mortified. She'd then taken pity on him and loaded him up with so much stuff he'd ended up dropping the colander on his toe on the way back up to the apartment—and it had been very heavy.

All right, so it hadn't been all bad. The grocery shopping had been kind of fun. Watching Mel measure up the tomatoes, check out all the different types of beans available and practise her abysmal French on the shopkeeper had turned him on, sort of. But his attempts to make her forget the whole cooking idea and go straight back to bed when they got to the apartment had been met with a frosty look.

'Now, the secret to omelettes is not to put the egg in the frying-pan until you can see smoke coming off it,' Mel prompted beside him.

She put her hand over his on the handle and tilted the pan so the butter slid across it. Her cheeks were flushed pink from the heat of the small kitchen as she bit her lip in concentration. Free of make-up, her face looked younger and even more sweet and appealing than usual. His annoyance seemed to melt away with the butter as he studied her.

She captivated him and he didn't know why.

Her enthusiasm at such a small thing as cooking at home on a cold December evening was infectious. She made even simple mundane tasks, things he'd never considered doing in the past, seem like an adventure. He shook his head, trying to dispel the thought. The homemaker gene was something he'd been born without. Thank the Lord. He wasn't about to start nurturing it now.

'Right, it's ready,' Mel said eagerly.

Jack jerked himself back to reality. 'Huh?'

Mel turned to see Jack frowning down at her. He looked confused and even a little annoyed. 'The pan, it's ready. You can put the eggs in now.'

'Oh, yeah.'

He picked up the egg mixture, splashed it into the pan. It gave a satisfying sizzle.

'Mmm.' Mel smiled as she inhaled the savoury scent. 'I love that smell. My dad used to cook us omelettes for breakfast on a Sunday morning after mass. There, you can turn it now.'

She guided his hand and together they folded the omelette, halved it and transferred it to the plates Mel had left warming under the grill. She sprinkled the food with fresh herbs and grabbed the bowl of green beans they'd prepared earlier.

'Let's eat in the living room,' she said, leading the way.

They sat cross-legged in front of the fireplace, their plates on the thick oak coffee-table. The buttery perfume of freshly cooked omelette filled the air as Jack uncorked the wine and poured them both a glass.

'Your old man's pretty handy in the kitchen, isn't he?' he said as he handed Mel the chilled Chardonnay.

The comment sounded casual, but Mel detected an edge in his voice.

'He is now, but back when we were kids all he could manage was omelettes. My Mum taught him how to cook those first. She says he was completely useless when they first met. My granny had mollycoddled him mercilessly.'

'Sounds like a lucky guy,' Jack murmured before eating a forkful of the eggs. 'Hey, this is delicious.'

'Don't sound so surprised.' Mel smiled, took a taste herself. 'Hmm, not bad, for a beginner.'

Mel watched as Jack polished off the food. Why had he never learned to cook before? Had his own mother spoilt him rotten too? He seemed so confident, so sure of himself, but somehow the picture didn't fit. Especially after what he'd said about his family at Christmas dinner.

'Didn't you learn anything from your own mum?' she asked, casually.

'Believe me, my mom was no Betty Crocker.' He gave a harsh laugh, tearing a piece of bread from the baguette on the table. 'She split on me when I was ten, but before that she was too busy feeding her habit to worry about feeding me.'

Mel felt the few bites of food she'd eaten turn over in her stomach. The carelessness of his statement making the content seem even uglier. The fire warmed her back, but she felt suddenly chilled. 'Your mother was a drug addict?'

It was a stupid question, Mel realised as soon as she'd said it.

His head came up. 'Yeah.' He dropped the bread on his plate, took a sip of wine. 'Among other things.' He put the glass back on the table, leaned against the couch. He looked relaxed, indifferent, but he hadn't taken his eyes off her. 'She turned tricks too. I can still remember the sound of her going at it while I pretended to be asleep on the couch. We only had two rooms, so she'd have to haul me out of bed in the middle of the night when she had company.' His lips curved, but there was no amusement in his eyes. 'That's what she called it—"company"—like she was some southern belle.'

'What happened to you when she left?'

Mel forced herself to ask the question, her heart pounding hard in her chest. Had he had any childhood at all?

He shrugged, turned to stare into the fire. 'She dumped me on her pimp. Hell, he may even have been my old man—she told me he was, but I don't think she knew for sure.'

'What was he like?'

He turned back to her. She could see the bitterness in his eyes. 'He was okay when he wasn't drinking. After he beat the hell out of me a couple of times I knew to beat it whenever he hit the bottle.'

She stiffened, unsure what to say. He wouldn't want her sympathy, she was sure of that, but she felt the rush of it all the same. How terrible it must have been for him, a child trying to make sense of something few adults could explain. She thought of the things he wrote about in his novels, the hard, desperate, grasping lives many of his characters led, and suddenly she understood why he could describe them so well.

The fire crackled in the grate, her food lay half-eaten on her plate. 'Did you ever see your mother again?' she asked at last.

He was still watching her, his eyes carefully blank now. 'She tracked me down once when I was in my teens. I was working at a truck stop. She wanted money. I told her to get lost.' His shoulder hitched. 'It wasn't exactly a Kodak moment.'

'Is that why you didn't want publicity? Because of what you came from?'

* * *

It was exactly the reason.

Jack straightened, the sofa hard against his back, suddenly wary.

Why had he told her so much? At first, he'd wanted to shock her, to make her see that this nice little domestic scene they had going would never last, not with someone like him. But she hadn't been shocked. He'd seen anguish in her eyes, compassion even, but there'd been none of the shock and disgust he would have expected.

A thought occurred to him and he felt ice skid up his spine. 'Just so you know. If any of this appears in print, I'll sue.'

He saw shock then; her face went deathly white. She looked as if she'd been slapped.

'I would never betray you like that.' Her voice was barely more than a whisper. She leaned forward and picked up his plate. 'I'll go wash these up.'

'Hey.' He reached forward, gripped her wrist. 'Don't take offence.'

She shrugged off his hand, stood up. 'How could I not take offence, Jack?'

Mel pushed her temper to the fore to cover the hurt. It wasn't hard. 'You don't just insult me when you say something like that, you know. You insult yourself. Do you really think I would sleep with you, let you confide in me and then put all the details in a magazine article?'

He stood up too, pulled the plates out of her hands. Her fingers were gripped so hard on Madame Marinez's china he had to tug them loose, before dumping them back on the table.

He smiled, making her temper flare again. 'You're not real thick-skinned, are you? For a reporter?' he said.

He lifted his hand up to touch her hair. She jerked back. 'Don't, Jack.'

'Okay, I'm sorry. I shouldn't have said that.'

She shook her head, feeling the sudden sting of tears. 'Jack, I'm not stupid. I know this isn't going anywhere. We're just having a good time while it lasts. I know that. I'm not looking for anything more than you are.' Maybe if she said it out loud she could believe it. 'But if you can't even trust me enough to know that I would never write about anything we did together in private, then I think we ought to end it now.'

'Come on, Cinders, don't get all melodramatic.' He slipped his hands round her waist, jostled her. She tried to step away but he held on. 'I do trust you,' he said, his voice deliberately light. 'And I'm sorry, really. I don't know what made me say it. I guess I felt kind of raw. I've never told anyone that stuff before.'

She softened against him, thinking about what he'd told her. 'You shouldn't be ashamed of your past, Jack.'

He gave a bitter laugh. 'That's easy for you to say.'

'I know it is. But you were a child; you didn't do anything wrong. It's not your fault where you came from.'

'I know,' he said. 'I just didn't want it to be public knowledge.' He let go of her, ran his hand through his hair. 'I had enough trouble growing up. Everyone in the town where I lived judged me because of them.' He sat down on the couch, looked up at her. 'It was always, that Jack's got bad blood, he'll come to no good. No matter what I did, no one ever wanted to give me a chance. I got out and went to New York. But when I sold that first manuscript, I didn't want it all coming back at me. And I sure as hell didn't want my mother turning up again.'

She sat beside him, rubbed a hand on his thigh. 'What made you change your mind? Decide to give the press conference?'

He put his hand on hers, looked round at her. 'You did.'

'Me!'

He chuckled. 'Yeah, I wanted to get your goat so bad, I called Eli and had him schedule the conference.' He turned her hand over in his, pressed his thumb into the palm. 'The deal was, I was gonna show you what you'd run out on.' He leaned back, still holding her hand, and gave her a self-dep-recating smile. 'Of course, I thought you were a reporter then—and you'd be devastated you'd missed out on the story of the year. Turned out the joke was on me, though, didn't it?'

'Serves you right,' she said, her own lips curving.

'I know.'

She took her hand away, studied it for a moment. 'Jack.' She raised her eyes to his. 'What will you do if your mother does turn up?'

'She won't.' He straightened and leaned forward, looking away from her as he rested his arms on his knees. 'I hired a detective a while back when it didn't look as though I was going to be able to keep ahead of the reporters forever. My plan was to pay her off, keep her out of my life. Turned out I didn't have to.' He shrugged, but she could see the stiffness in his shoulders. 'She died ten years ago. Drugs overdose.'

'I'm sorry, Jack.'

He looked back at her. 'Don't be. She doesn't—' He stopped, corrected himself. 'She didn't mean a thing to me.'

Somehow, she doubted that was true, but knew she didn't have the right to say so. There was one thing, though, that she wanted to get straight between them.

'I want you to know, Jack. Whatever Dansworth may want, I'm not going to write about your personal life in this article.'

He sat up, his eyes sharpened, but he didn't speak.

'I'd like to talk to you about your work,' she continued. 'And that's what I'm going to concentrate on. You can look at the article, once it's finished. If there's anything you object to, I'll cut it out.'

'Hey.' Bracing one hand on the back of the sofa, he tucked a finger under her chin. 'You don't have to do that.'

'I want to,' she said simply, and meant it.

He might want to trust her, she thought, but she doubted trust was easy for him after the experiences of his childhood.

She'd come to like him a lot in the last few days. They'd had fun, but, more than that, they'd become friends, and she wasn't about to jeopardise that for some silly magazine article.

CHAPTER TWELVE

'WHAT'S wrong?' Mel asked, unable to take her eyes off the rigid line of Jack's jaw.

'Nothing,' came the clipped response as he stared out the plane window, his fingers drumming against the seat divider.

Mel could see his Adam's apple bobbing up and down as he swallowed. His skin looked pale and drawn beneath his tan. Why wouldn't he tell her what was bothering him?

The first-class hostess leaned across Mel. 'Mr Devlin, you need to fasten your seat belt now. We're only a few minutes from take-off.'

Jack's head jerked round. 'What?'

'You need to fasten your seat belt, Mr Devlin.'

He reached for the belt. Mel noticed his hands tremble as he clicked it closed.

So did the stewardess. 'Is everything okay, Mr Devlin?'

'Yeah, everything's dandy,' he said. The sarcasm bristled as he turned back to the window.

'Don't forget to press the call button if there's anything you need,' the stewardess replied.

Jack ignored her, his foot now tapping in time with his fingers.

The hostess gave Mel an unsteady smile before walking off to continue her pre-flight passenger check.

He'd been rude and obnoxious, which was unlike him.

Mel's concern increased. Something was definitely wrong and she intended to find out what.

She settled her hand over his. He tensed as his head whipped round, but his fingers stilled at last. 'I'm okay,' he said. 'Stop bugging me.'

He pulled his hand away, but not before she felt how cool and clammy it was.

'No, you're not,' she said patiently. 'You haven't been okay since we got up this morning.'

He braced as the low rumble of the plane's engines started and his eyes darted out the window. Suddenly she knew what the problem was.

'Are you scared of flying?'

'Don't be dumb,' he said, his eyes still fixed on the tarmac. 'I fly all the time.' His body was as stiff as the seat back behind him. 'I just don't like it much, that's all.'

Jack struggled to swallow the surge of nausea as he saw the tarmac roll beneath them. If this damn tin bird didn't get in the air soon, he was liable to throw up all over himself.

Normally he would have taken several sedatives and a shot of whiskey and been happily numb through the whole experience, but when he woke that morning, Mel curled against his side, pride had got the better of him. It was only the take-off that gave him big problems and he didn't want Mel knowing he needed to be virtually unconscious to get through it. He figured he'd just grin and bear it this time. How bad could it be?

Pretty damn catastrophic, it seemed, now that he was approaching zero hour in complete control of his faculties. He might very well lose what little breakfast he'd managed to get down.

The muscles in his neck screamed in protest as he tried to ease his head back. The air clogged in his lungs. He couldn't breathe properly. The plane juddered as it swung in a turn towards the runway and his stomach lurched right along with it.

His voice cracked out on a muffled curse, sounding shaky even to him.

Warm fingers settled on his neck and began to massage the rock-solid muscles. 'Relax, Jack—and try to breathe.'

Her voice sounded blessedly calm, even though Jack could barely hear it over the roaring in his ears.

'I can't,' he said stupidly, the panic taking over as the plane began to pick up speed. He squeezed his eyes shut, gripping the seat rests as the world shuddered around him and his body pressed back into the seat. He was going to die.

Gentle fingers gripped his chin and pulled his head around. 'Open your eyes.' The sharp command had them snapping open. He looked into eyes dark with concern. 'Now look at me and breathe with me,' she said.

Her hands felt cool on his neck, caressing the knotted muscles.

'Take your hands off the seat and hold onto me.' He grabbed her waist, pushing his hands beneath the wool of her jumper. The bare skin beneath felt soft and warm, and secure. That seductive scent of hers made him think of her naked and willing beneath him as she had been the night before. His breath finally released in an unsteady rush.

'And again, breathe, Jack.' He sucked the air back in greedily, let it out as she began to count softly in his ear, her fingers stroking his neck, making the hair on his nape tingle with an awareness that had nothing to do with his fear. 'You're all right, Jack. I'm with you, okay?'

'Okay.' He grunted the word, his lungs sore, but the breaths still coming in jerky gasps.

The plane lurched into the air and his chest seized up again. Clammy sweat trickled down his back and his body shook as the hum of the engines thundered in his ears.

'I'm still with you, Jack.'

He pushed his hands further up her back, under her clothes, clinging to her and struggling to concentrate on the texture of her skin, soft and reassuring under his fingers. He tried hard to ignore the weightlessness low in his belly as the plane lifted away from the ground. Her hands settled on his cheeks, pushing him back to reality, forcing him away from that brittle edge of fear. Then her lips were on his, her tongue sliding along the crease of his rigidly closed mouth.

'Kiss me,' she whispered.

Arousal slammed into him as he opened his mouth and covered hers, taking what she offered like a starving man.

Mel trembled as Jack's fingers dug into her back and he dragged her against him. The armrest pressed hard into her belly, but she could barely feel it. All her thoughts, all her feelings, were concentrated on his mouth, his lips as they devoured her. He pulled back for a moment, his breath and hers rasping out.

'What the…?' He sounded dazed.

Her fingers fisted in his hair and she pulled him back to her. His body shook as the kiss went deeper. His tongue delving and then retreating making her yearn for more. The low throbbing at her core became more insistent, her insides burning. The snap of her bra releasing heaved her back to reality. His palms cupped her breasts under the sweater, the thumbs rubbing over the hard peaks and making her shake.

'Stop, we can't…' Her fevered mind grasped for the words but couldn't find them as he continued to caress her breasts, his lips nibbling at the pulse in her neck forcing her head back against the seat.

The loud ping and the sound of the stewardess telling them the seat-belt sign had been switched off had barely registered when Jack released her suddenly. She watched, her mind still disconnected from her body as he snapped off his own belt, then unfastened hers. Standing up, he grabbed her hand, pulled her up on shaking legs. The fierce passion swirling in his eyes as he stared at her made the pulse at her core throb harder. 'Come on,' he said.

She stumbled behind him, her hand gripped tight in his, down the wide aisle of the first-class cabin. Her breasts bounced beneath her sweater and she folded an arm across herself, trying to disguise their unfettered state as Jack slammed into the washroom and pulled her in behind him.

The door banged against the frame and he snapped the lock shut, the sharp click ricocheting like a gunshot.

She grabbed hold of his shoulders as he lifted her onto the wide shelf next to the sink. 'Jack, stop it. We can't—'

'The hell we can't,' he said as he shoved her sweater and bra up, exposing her heaving breasts. The harsh need in his voice shocked her, but the sizzle of excitement wasn't far behind. She'd never made love in a public place before. But as her mind registered the thought his mouth settled hot on her breast, his teeth tugging at the engorged nipple, and all coherent thought fled.

Her mind reeled with the hot surge of passion as his hands thrust under her skirt. He forced it up past her waist, then swiftly dragged down her knickers, shredding her tights as he pulled them off. She felt the cool tiles against her bare bottom, the warmth of his palms as he grasped her hips and pressed the hard ridge in his jeans to her centre. He fumbled briefly, cursed loudly and then the hard velvet head prodded against her sex.

'Wrap your legs around me,' he rasped. She clung to his shoulders, desperate to feel his heat, his hardness inside her. He lifted her easily, impaling her on the rigid length. She moaned, the pressure immense as he pushed into the slick folds. Settling her back on the tiles, he pushed her thighs wide, anchored her bottom with strong hands and began to thrust, hard and fast, forcing her to take the full measure of him. The pleasure built like wildfire. She cried out, the flames flaring at her breasts, beating molten at her core as the inferno burst inside her.

The pleasure didn't dim. Wave upon wave engulfed her as he got larger, harder inside her, forcing her to take more, to want more. 'I can't… It's too much.' The words came out on a broken sob as the pleasure surged up still further. Her whole body shook as it raced towards that unbearable peak.

His grunts matched her cries of fulfilment as they tumbled over together.

The jolt of turbulence brought Jack sharply back to reality. He tensed, but the sudden bolt of fear didn't come. He could smell her, the musty scent of sex and the fresh, familiar perfume she wore. Her arms were limp around his shoulder, her breath coming in shattered gasps where her face was nuzzled against his neck. He eased himself out of her, assailed by a wave of guilt when he felt her flinch.

He'd taken her like an animal. He'd barely even stopped to see if she was ready for him, before thrusting into her like a madman. With the frenzy of arousal and adrenaline past, shame replaced it in a chilling rush.

'I'm sorry, Mel.' He stroked her hips, sure he'd left bruises on her soft skin.

'Hmm?' The muffled murmur sounded almost like a purr. Jack wasn't convinced.

Taking her arms as gently as he could, he held her away from him. Noticing the redness of whisker burns around her nipples, he pulled her bra back down with clumsy fingers, then smoothed the sweater over her bosom. He settled his hands on her waist and forced himself to look her in the eye. 'Are you okay?'

Her pupils were dark and dilated, her lips red and a little puffy from the roughness of his kisses. She looked shattered.

'Mel, did I hurt you?' he asked again, more insistent now. He swallowed, the fear almost choking him. Had she told him to stop? He couldn't even remember, he thought, horrified with himself.

She cocked her head to one side, looking confused. 'Don't be ridiculous, Jack. Of course you didn't hurt me.' Her lips curved, making him blink. 'In fact, I think I may have just had the most phenomenal orgasm of my life.'

The surge of relief was so intense his knees trembled. 'Mel, I don't know what the hell happened,' he blurted out, unable to push the guilt away completely. He'd never taken a woman like that before, with such urgency, such desperation. 'One minute I was clinging onto you, sure I was about to die, the next I was inside you pounding away like a lunatic.' The words flooded out as he touched his forehead to hers, held her gently. Still a little scared she might break.

'Yes, well.' She leaned back, stroked a palm down his cheek, the mischievous twinkle in her eye making him grateful all over again. 'It was certainly a novel way to cure you of your fear of flying.'

'I don't have a fear of…' The denial died on his lips when her eyebrow winged up, challenging him to continue. 'All right, okay, so maybe it does freak me out a little.'

He stepped back, concentrated on sorting out his own clothing, knowing he couldn't talk about it now.

Mel looked at his bowed head and felt her heart melt. She'd never seen him like this before. So raw, so needy.

The smell of sex was still heavy in the air around them, and she felt a little tender from the roughness of their coupling. But she wouldn't have changed it for anything. They'd made love as if their lives depended on it—and she hadn't been joking when she'd told him it was the most earth-shattering orgasm she'd ever experienced. They'd made love with abandon before, but he'd never lost control like that. Mel knew an important barrier had been broken down between them and she was sure he knew it too, that was why he couldn't look at her now. She didn't understand, though, why she didn't feel as wary as he did. She couldn't afford to get in any deeper than he could. But somehow it didn't seem to matter any more. She reached out and touched his hair.

His head came up, the wary look in his eyes unmistakable.

'You don't have to be embarrassed about it. Not with me,' she said quietly.

'I know. But I don't feel much like talking about it.'

The dismissal stung a little, but Mel forced herself to let the hurt go. She had no right to pry into his thoughts, his feelings.

'We better get out of here,' Jack said, carefully. 'Before someone figures out what we've been doing.' He put his hand on Mel's thigh, squeezed and let go. 'You sure you're okay?'

'Yes.' She blushed, suddenly very aware of where they were and what they'd just done. She'd die of embarrassment if anyone in the first-class cabin figured it out. 'I need to clean up a little, though.' She got down off the vanity and turned to the sink.

He dropped her knickers and the remnants of her tights on the surface beside her as she turned on the tap.

'Look,' he said from behind her. 'I didn't use a condom. Is that going to be a problem?'

Mel swallowed, her throat suddenly dry. The thought hadn't even occurred to her.

'I don't know,' she said truthfully.

He took her arm, pulled her round to face him. 'You're not on the pill?'

She shook her head.

'When was your last period?'

The blunt question made even more colour flush into Mel's cheeks. 'Before Christmas. About a week before Christmas.'

He rubbed a hand down his face, sighed. 'That puts us smack in the middle of your cycle.' He paused, obviously considering the options. 'I want you to let me know if there are any consequences. We'll sort it out together, okay?'

Mel suddenly had the overwhelming urge to cry. A life could be starting inside her and he was talking clinically about consequences. She tugged her arm out of his grasp, turned back to the sink. 'Don't worry about it. I doubt there will be any consequences.'

'But if there are, I want to know about it.'

She nodded, unable to look at him. The statement sounded so final, somehow, so abrupt. She'd just realised she was falling in love and he was already planning to leave.

'Good. I better sneak out first. Don't forget to lock the door behind me,' he said. His hand touched her hair in a brief caress and then he was gone.

A tear slipped down her cheek as she heard the door close.

She wiped the tear away, turned and clicked the lock. She pulled some paper towels from the vanity unit above the sink with unsteady hands, began soaking them in the hot soapy water.

She'd been a complete fool. She'd only gone and fallen in love with him. He was probably at this very moment trying to think of ways to disentangle himself from her.

She blew out a breath, carefully began to swab herself with the towels, cleaning his seed away. And just to turn a crisis into a disaster, she might be pregnant to boot. Her hands shook. She wouldn't think about that until it happened. But somehow the knowledge she would be alone by the time she knew for sure, made the prospect even harder to face.

Mel returned to her seat, absurdly conscious of the eyes of the other passengers as she walked down the aisle. When she had settled into her seat and fastened her belt, Jack took her hand.

He rubbed his thumb over the back of it before raising her fingers to his lips.

'Don't look so worried, Cinders.' The silly nickname made her heart lurch. Why couldn't he just be horrible now, so when they parted it would be easier? 'Whatever happens, we'll figure it out.'

He relaxed back into his seat, an oddly contented smile on his lips, and promptly fell asleep, his hand still holding hers.

Once his breathing had become slow and steady, Mel pulled her hand loose. She needed to start establishing some distance between them. She'd had her fun, and she would have to pay the consequences. And a broken heart might turn out to be the least of her worries. But one thing was for sure. She wasn't going to let him dictate the terms of the relationship any more. She needed to protect herself now. They had a week scheduled in New York and then four days in LA.

She turned to look at him, his black hair tousled and his handsome face almost boyish in sleep. If she were being really rational, really sensible, she would end it straight away. But somehow she couldn't bring herself to do it. The next week and a half would be painfully bittersweet, but, as long as she knew what was coming, she could prepare herself for it and get the most out of it she possibly could.

CHAPTER THIRTEEN

MEL awoke the next morning to an empty bed. Stretching across the huge mattress, she could feel the cold space beside her where Jack should have been. She'd become so used to having him wrapped around her when she woke, she felt oddly disorientated. The seven-hour time difference probably didn't help.

Giving a huge yawn, she peeked out from under the duvet and studied the master bedroom. She'd been groggy and exhausted the night before and had barely glanced at the room or its furnishings before stumbling into bed with Jack. They'd both been so tired, they hadn't even had the energy to make love. He'd held her instead, tucking her against his lean, muscular body. She remembered his hand stroking her hair back from her face, the buzz of his lips against her cheek as she fell asleep. The memory made her smile.

The floor-to-ceiling picture window on the far side of the room afforded a spectacular view of Central Park at dawn. The sun was already making its presence felt, halos of red and orange bleeding into the night sky on the horizon.

Pushing herself up on the stack of fluffy pillows, Mel yawned again, then glanced at the clock on the bedside table. Seven o'clock in the morning New York time. Blimey, she'd slept like the dead, for a solid twelve hours. But where was Jack?

She sighed, stretched and then flipped the duvet back. The waking sun cast a dim light on a large canvas on the opposite wall. All harsh lines and bright colours, the painting looked striking but impersonal.

As Mel wandered into the bathroom—again daringly modern with grey granite tiles and gleaming steel fixtures— she noted the complete absence of any personal features there too, apart from Jack's damp towel that had been thrown over the heated towel-rail. She shook her head as she straightened it. Why could guys never fold anything properly? All four of her brothers had the same affliction.

After a scalding hot shower, Mel applied some moisturiser and slipped into her oldest pair of jeans and a skin-tight T-shirt. Determined to feel as comfortable as possible while she went in search of Jack.

The unsettling feeling increased, though, as she walked through the vaulted open-plan living room, the feature aspect of which was another wall of glass looking out onto the park. Just as in Jack's Parisian apartment there were no photographs on the walls, no mementoes on the shelves, no magazines on the coffee-table, no knick-knacks or clutter anywhere. Of course, he'd been away for a while, but she wondered if this could possibly be his main home. She'd assumed it must be, but now she wasn't so sure. How could a person live somewhere and leave so little of themself there?

Mel had inspected three more bedrooms, all as expertly designed, luxuriously furnished and utterly soulless as the rest of the apartment, before she heard a faint tapping coming from a room at the end of the hallway.

She walked soundlessly to the doorway, her bare feet sinking into the thick carpeting. This room at least had one wall lined with daunting-looking textbooks to add a bit of character. Jack sat at the large desk opposite the bookshelves, hunched over a computer keyboard. The early-morning light lit his face in profile as his fingers flew across the keys. The only piece of clothing he had on were a disreputable pair of sweat pants. He paused for a moment, concentrated intently on the screen, and then bent his head, bowed his shoulders and started typing again. She guessed he had been there for quite a while because his hair was dry and furrowed where he must have combed his fingers through it.

Mel had never seen him work before and was fascinated. He seemed so absorbed. She could see it wasn't an easy process for him, though, from the harsh frown on his face.

He stopped abruptly and looked across at her. 'Hey, you're up.' His voice sounded rusty.

'Yes. I'm sorry, I didn't mean to disturb you.'

'That's okay.' He leaned back, scrubbed his fingers through his hair. 'The first wave's passing anyway.'

'I could go out and get us some breakfast, if you want to carry on working,' she said, feeling like an intruder.

He held out an arm towards her. 'Come here,' he said, beckoning with his fingers.

When she walked up to him, he wrapped his arm round her hips and pressed his head into her side. 'I like having you here.' The simple words dispelled the uneasy feeling that had been dogging Mel ever since she'd woken up.

'I like being here,' she said, sliding her hands over the firm muscles of his shoulders. He sank his face into the soft cotton of her T-shirt and took a deep breath.

She meant it, she realised—whatever doubts she might have, whatever fears, she loved being here with him.

He lifted his head, looked up at her. 'You smell great,' he murmured; the appreciation in his eyes made her belly tighten. 'How about I buy you breakfast?' He let her go and stood up. 'Nowhere does breakfast better than New York. And I'm in the mood to celebrate.'

'What are we celebrating?' Mel said, feeling light-headed

as he clasped her hand and led her towards the door, his enthusiasm evident in every stride.

'I'll tell you as soon as we're both sitting with a stack of pancakes in front of us drowned in maple syrup.' He patted his flat belly, glanced back at her and grinned. 'I've been writing for four hours and I'm starving.'

'You're always starving,' she said, grinning back at him.

The misty light cast a cold, frosty spell over Central Park as they strolled across it. Jack squeezed Mel's hand, loving the soft, sure feel of her fingers in his as he took a bracing breath of the chilled air, watched the white cloud plume out in front of him.

He couldn't have felt better right now if he had just invented a cure for cancer, brought about world peace and slayed a few hundred dragons—all at the same time.

He was writing again. He hadn't realised how much it had been bothering him, until the huge gush of relief when he'd sat down this morning and the words had flowed through his head again—and straight onto the computer screen.

And he knew it was all because of Mel. His life had been stagnating for years. The writing had just been the last thing to go. As soon as Mel had walked into it, that night at The Ritz, she'd given it purpose again. He didn't know how she had and he didn't know why she had, but he wasn't about to question it. She was his muse now, he was sure of it, and he wasn't about to let her go. He guessed that was selfish of him, but he didn't care.

He spotted his favourite diner nestled among the imposing brownstones as they exited the park. He couldn't think of anything he'd rather do now than eat pancakes, drink scalding coffee and look at her.

He lifted her hand in his and pointed at the tiny neighbourhood restaurant across the street. 'I hope you're hungry, because you're in for the best breakfast of your life.'

* * *

Mel dropped her napkin onto the table and groaned. 'I'm so stuffed I think you're going to have to roll me out of here. I must have gained about ten pounds in the last week.'

Jack looked up from shovelling down his second helping of pancakes and bacon. After leaning round the table to give her a quick once-over he shook his head. 'Nu-uh, you could still stand to gain a few pounds.'

'What?'

'You're still a little skinny on the hips. I like my women with more to hold onto.'

'Oh, you do, do you?' She picked her napkin up and threw it at him. 'You cheeky devil.'

He pushed the plate away and settled back, his long legs bumping hers under the table. The skin round his eyes crinkled playfully. 'The way I figure it, you were at your fighting weight at The Ritz. You lost some after. Won't do you any harm at all to get it back again.'

'But I was fat,' she said, trying to sound indignant but enjoying the glow of approval in his eyes.

'Well, now,' he said. He wiped his mouth with the napkin she'd thrown at him. 'I guess I like you fat, then.'

'That's the wrong answer,' she said, in no doubt that the big grin on her face told him it was exactly the right answer. 'You're supposed to say I wasn't fat, I was thin.'

No one had ever given her a more perfect compliment. She hadn't realised how much Adam's niggling reminders she could stand to lose a few pounds had continued to undermine her confidence until now.

'You weren't thin,' he replied, lifting her hand off the table, studying it as he turned it over. 'You were voluptuous.' Bending his head, he nipped his teeth into the pad of flesh at the base of her thumb.

Her pulse spiked in surprise and arousal.

'And thank goodness you still are.' He waggled his other hand. 'Give or take a couple of pounds.'

She took her hand out of his, not sure it was wise to feel quite so excited in a public place. The last time that had happened they'd ended up making love at twenty thousand feet. But she couldn't resist saying: 'Exactly how big do you think the toilet is here?'

He threw back his head and laughed, making her face blaze with colour. Good God, had she really said that? Why didn't she just pull off her knickers now and go sit in his lap?

'I like the way your mind works, lady,' he said, throwing a twenty-dollar bill onto the table. He stood up, took her hand and hauled her out of the booth. 'But they probably would arrest us if we tried it here. Americans can be fussy about that sort of thing. Let's get home. Fast.'

They were lying back in the big bed together, the brittle mid-morning sunlight illuminating the clothes strewn across the floor, when Mel propped herself up on Jack's chest. The hum of great sex was still heating her blood, but her mind was at last starting to clear of the sexual fog that had been hazing it ever since they'd raced back across the park from the diner.

'I forgot to ask what we were celebrating?'

'Hmm, now, let me see,' Jack said, his eyes closed as his hand stroked her bare backside. 'I think I was celebrating your nice plump little butt.'

He gave the butt in question a hefty pat.

She gasped, then yanked one of his chest hairs.

'Ouch!' His eyes flew open. 'What was that for?'

'It's not plump, it's voluptuous, remember?' She folded her arms over his chest, propped her chin on them, satisfied that she'd got his attention now. 'And anyhow, that's not what you were talking about earlier. When I found you in your study,' she prompted.

'Oh, yeah.' He snuggled into the bed, closed his eyes and rested his hands back on her bottom. 'I got started on my next manuscript, managed to get out thirty pages this morning,' he said, a satisfied smile on his face.

'Is that good, then?'

He opened his eyes at her question. 'Honey, that's not just good, it's phenomenal. I haven't written more than a page in close to three months. It's been killing me.'

She sat up, unable to hide the surprise in her voice. 'But that's, that's terrible.' It never would have occurred to her that someone as successful as he was would suffer from something as mundane as writer's block. 'Does it happen to you a lot?'

'Not a lot, no. It's happened before, but nowhere near as bad as that.' He put a hand behind his head, his eyes intent on her. 'I couldn't seem to find a way out of it this time. It was really bugging me, until you turned up in my hotel bathroom.'

'Me?' Okay, now she wasn't just surprised, she was astonished.

'Yeah, after that, not being able to write a word didn't bug me nearly as much as you did.' He raised one eyebrow mischievously.

'Well, thanks a lot.'

He chuckled. 'You know what, I forgot all about it. Getting you into bed and then onto the book tour and then back into bed again and stopping you running off in between took up all my time and energy. You're a heck of a lot of work, you know that, Cinders?'

'And worth every second of it,' she replied, haughtily.

'You won't get an argument from me there,' he said, his fingers trailing up her arm and curling around her nape. He tugged her down to him, kissed her gently. Her breasts brushed the hair of his chest, the contact making them harden.

She lifted her head as his fingers let go of her neck, looked into eyes bright with amusement and deepened by desire.

His lips tilted up in a confidential smile as his thumb traced the line of her neck, then dipped lower to circle her nipple. 'I woke up this morning and the words were all just there again, right where I wanted them.' His eyes came back to hers at her sharp intake of breath. 'Just like you were. You're good for me, Cinders.'

Mel felt her heart plunge that last little bit of the way into love. 'You're good for me too, Jack,' she murmured against his lips, before sinking into the kiss.

Once the book signing and the question and answer session were out of the way on the first day—a gruelling three-hour ordeal at a flagship bookstore on Sixth Avenue—their time was their own. They only had a few days left in New York, but Mel intended to make the most of every second. Getting into a routine with Jack was going to be a bittersweet experience—the thought of how she was going to cope when they parted never far from her mind.

They had such a great time together, not just in bed, but out of it too. Surely he could see that. He took her to the Metropolitan Opera House the first night. But the chauffeur-driven limo, the champagne on ice waiting in their private box weren't as enchanting for Mel as the time she got to spend alone with him. Walking in the park in the afternoon, their footfalls marked in the freshly fallen snow. A trip to the grocery store to buy a bag of Oreos and a quart of milk, so Jack could survive until suppertime while they watched a Giants game on the huge plasma TV in his living room. The everyday tasks gave their relationship an intimacy that thrilled Mel—although she knew she'd never get the hang of American football.

He whisked her off to Saks Fifth Avenue on the afternoon of New Year's Eve on the pretext he had to buy himself a suit for a party his US agent wanted him to attend. It wasn't until that evening Mel discovered his true purpose when he draped a clothes bag with a designer logo across her lap.

She picked up the package, looking up from the computer where she had been working on her article. 'What's this?'

'Your outfit for tonight.' Fresh from his shower with a towel slung low on his hips, he rubbed his wet hair with a towel. 'It just got here. You better go get ready.'

'But I thought we agreed I wouldn't go.' She didn't want to expose their relationship to public scrutiny—and she was sure he didn't either. They'd only narrowly avoided being snapped by the paparazzi at the opera the night before. He'd managed to cover both their faces with his coat but afterwards in the car she'd been able to see the intrusion had angered him.

'No, we didn't,' he replied, slinging the towel over his shoulder. 'You said you didn't have anything to wear.' He nodded at the bag, ran his hand through his hair. 'Now you do.'

Jack waited for her response, and tried not to look as frustrated as he felt.

He couldn't figure out what he was doing wrong.

He'd been working his butt off the last day and a half laying on the romance. He'd even taken her to the opera—which had bored him stiff—and still she hadn't asked him if she could stick around when the book tour finished.

Damn, he'd never had to work this hard before. In fact, he'd never had to work at all. But ever since he'd made up his mind she had to stay with him, things just hadn't worked out how they were supposed to.

And then, to top it all, this morning she'd come up with some dumb excuse not to spend New Year's Eve with him. It had totally stumped him. Apart from the fact that he knew he'd never survive the party without her there, he couldn't understand why she'd want to stay home alone. He'd been forced to take desperate measures. He'd dragged her to Saks, had got one of the shop assistants to work out her size for him and had even gone through the torture of picking out a dress for her himself an hour later while she'd been busy buying presents for her family.

If she said no now, he'd lose it completely.

'You bought me something to wear?' She sounded amazed.

'Yeah, now go get it on, the limo's due here in half an hour.'

'But, Jack.' She looked up at him. He was stunned to see the sheen of tears in her eyes. 'You said it was a celebrity party. There'll probably be reporters and photographers there.'

'What's your point?' His frustration edged up another notch.

'You don't mind?'

'About what?'

'About the publicity. They might photograph us together.'

'No, I don't mind. Why, do you?' Didn't she want to be seen with him? The thought hadn't even occurred to him, but, now that it had, it bothered him, big time.

'Of course *I* don't mind.'

'Well, good,' he said, relief gushing through him. 'I'm real glad we got that settled.' He cupped her elbow, pulled her out of the chair. 'Now go get the dress on.'

The soft smile that lit her face made his heart jump.

'All right, if you're sure you don't mind,' she said, hugging the garment bag against her chest.

'What I'll mind a lot more,' he said, giving her a gentle pat as she headed towards the bedroom, 'is going without you.'

CHAPTER FOURTEEN

MEL felt like Cinderella attending her ball as she stepped out of the limo and onto the dark blue carpet at The Ritz-Carlton's entrance. The strapless velvet dress she wore was simple, elegant, exquisitely chic and fitted her perfectly. She'd never felt more beautiful, but what made it special was the fact that Jack had bought it for her.

Was it really so ridiculous to think that he might come to love her, too? Maybe she ought to say something to him tonight about how she felt?

The winter air chilled her ankles as Jack led her past the phalanx of photographers, his hand firm on her back beneath the faux-fur wrap, which had been in the garment bag along with the dress. The bulbs flashed, but he didn't even flinch as he escorted her into the hotel's lobby.

'See,' he whispered in her ear as he took the wrap from her. 'That wasn't so hard, was it?' She could hear the smile in his voice.

It was already ten o'clock and the hotel's grand ballroom thronged with Manhattan's élite, done out in their finery and ready to ring in the New Year in style. Deluxe decorations of gold and silver accented the art deco columns while jewelled lights winked around them adding to the fairy-tale air. Through the terrace doors at the end of the room she could see the Statue of Liberty, standing proud in a shaft of light across the bay. A jazz quartet played in the corner, glasses clinked, conversations hummed, diamonds sparkled and famous faces mingled with faces Mel was convinced ought to be famous.

Many of the guests were fans of Jack's writing and, in their warm, bold American way, had no qualms at all about coming up and telling him so. She could tell by the way he kept her hand clutched in his the whole time, he wasn't all that thrilled with the attention. She sipped champagne and did her best not to smile at his discomfort. It didn't look as if they were going to get much chance to talk about anything tonight, but she didn't care. The knowledge she was here, in this exhilarating city, with this gorgeous man was making her quite giddy enough, thank you.

'Mel, wow, what a fantastic dress.'

Mel turned away from Jack, who was mired in conversation with a congressman from Queens, to see Alicia standing behind her, a cocktail glass in her hand and her eyes twinkling with appreciation as she scanned Mel's outfit.

'Thanks,' Mel said warmly, glad to finally see someone she knew. 'It's so good to see you again.' They'd shared a coffee together at the book signing the day before, so Alicia could brief her on some of the statistics of Jack's publishing history for the article, but had ended up nattering away about London clubs and pubs instead. Mel had been grateful Alicia hadn't brought up the subject of her personal relationship with Jack.

'I'm on a mission to find the Ladies,' Alicia said brightly. 'Do you want to join me?'

'Yes, please. I'll just tell Jack.'

After saying a quick hello to Alicia, Jack was reluctant to let Mel go. 'Don't be too long, okay?' he said, running his finger down her face. 'It's only twenty minutes to midnight, then we're out of here.'

Mel followed Alicia through the crowd, wondering if the

PR woman would comment on the intimate exchange. It didn't take her long to find out.

'So, is he as good in bed as everyone says?'

The burning hit Mel's cheeks as her eyes met Alicia's in the washroom mirror. 'Excuse me?'

Alicia smiled, her eyes warm and amused. 'Don't get embarrassed. It's pretty obvious you two have got it together in a big way.'

'It is?'

Mel didn't know who she was trying to fool. Of course it was obvious.

'I'm pea-green with envy, if you must know,' Alicia said, padding her freshly applied lipstick with a tissue. 'He's so hot.'

'Yes, he is.' What else could she say?

Alicia's voice sobered. She tucked her lipstick back inside her purse. 'Look, I don't really know how to say this.'

'Say what?' Why did Alicia look so serious all of a sudden?

'I mean, it's absolutely none of my business, but you seem really nice and I think we hit it off a bit on the Eurostar and at the book signing.'

'I had a good time,' Mel said, dully. The wave of optimism that had buoyed her up ever since Jack handed her the dress started to dissolve. Where on earth was this going?

'It's just…' Alicia looked down at the marble vanity unit, then back at Mel '…Jack's got a reputation as a bit of heartbreaker.'

'He has?' She knew she sounded like an idiot, but couldn't help it, she felt as if her chest had just deflated.

'I've got a friend called Catherine who used to work at Dark Knight,' Alicia continued. 'She was one of the copy editors. She had a brief fling with Jack about a year ago—she's still not quite over it.'

'What happened?' The question spilled out even though Mel was sure she didn't want the answer to it.

'He wasn't horrible or anything. I mean, he made it quite

clear to Cath right from the start that he wasn't interested in anything permanent.' Which was exactly what he'd done with her, Mel thought. 'But you know what it's like. You always think you can change a guy's mind. And she fell head over heels in love. As soon as she told him, though, that was the end of it.'

'He dumped her?'

'Not to put too fine a point on it. Yes, he did. He was sweet about it. Gave her all that rubbish about it wasn't her, it was him, but, frankly, I think he couldn't get away from her fast enough. And she was devastated. She had to move jobs eventually, because she was worried she might bump into him.'

'How is she now?'

Alicia's lips curved in a wry smile. 'She's a lot better. All the publicity before Christmas about him was pretty tough, but she's started dating again—which is the main thing. Look, I know it's none of my business, and whatever you and Jack have going might be completely different, but I'd hate to see any woman go through what Cath went through. I just wanted to warn you.'

'Thanks, but there's no need. I'm not the hopeless romantic type.' Mel heard herself saying the words, but knew they weren't true. 'And I've already figured out Jack isn't either.' How had she managed to lose sight of that? she thought.

'Phew!' Alicia smiled again. 'I'm so glad. It's just, the way he looks at you. It's pretty potent. It takes a strong woman to resist that.'

'Don't worry, really, I'll be fine.' Mel said the words, but she didn't feel them.

It was only ten minutes to midnight as she made her way back across the ballroom. She felt a little shaky, but wanted to get back to Jack, more determined than ever to make the most of the little time they had left.

Then a pudgy man in a tuxedo stepped in front of her. 'You're Carmel Rourke, right?' he said.

'Yes,' she replied, trying to hide her impatience.

'The English reporter who's doing the article on Devlin?'

'Yes, that's correct.' Who was this man? 'Excuse me, but do I know you?'

'You ought to, sweetheart,' he said. His chest puffed up, making him look like a penguin. 'I'm Donovan Delaney, society columnist for *The Post*.'

'That's nice,' Mel said, her eyes straying across the ballroom. She spotted Jack, who seemed to be searching for her. 'I'm sorry, but I need to go.'

'Hey, I just want a quick word,' the man said, sounding affronted.

'What about?' She didn't know what he wanted and she really didn't care, Jack was waiting for her.

'You must have heard the rumours about Devlin. Wondered what you know about it. You guys have been pretty close for the last week or so.'

'What rumours?' He had her attention now.

He smiled, the gleam in his eyes making him look more like a shark now than a penguin. 'Your boyfriend's got a real seedy past. Or so they're saying. You know anything about it?'

Mel felt anger and indignation surge through her. How dared he pry into Jack's private life and pass judgement when he knew nothing about it? 'I hardly think his past has anything to do with his work, which is all anyone's entitled to comment on.'

'Hey, sweetheart. Don't get snippy. It was only a little question.'

She excused herself as politely as she could, but as she walked away from him she wondered at the sharp smile on his face. It gave her the chills. Once she was by Jack's side, though, she forgot all about the annoying little man.

As the band counted down to the New Year, fireworks exploding in the bay as Lady Liberty joined the party, Mel clung onto Jack. He kissed her hard and long, his hands making her tremble as they caressed the exposed skin of her spine. When the kiss finally ended, he nuzzled her neck and whispered, 'Happy New Year, Cinders.'

She swallowed down the emotion lodged in her throat.

Don't you dare cry, she told herself. You've got him for another few nights at least, and you are not going to ruin it with stupid dreams that can never come true.

CHAPTER FIFTEEN

'I HAVE to go home, Jack.'

'What?' Jack's eyes lifted from the computer screen, re-focused on Mel.

'That was a call from my editor.' Mel bit her lip, struggling to keep the turmoil of emotions Dansworth's call had caused out of her voice. 'She wants the article finished and in her hand by the end of tomorrow.'

Jack turned off the laptop and closed the lid. 'But that's dumb. We've still got LA next week.'

'She thinks I've got more than enough information now to write a good piece.' Dansworth had ranted and raved at Mel for close to ten minutes. 'Dansworth...' Mel swallowed, not sure how to continue. 'She saw the paparazzi pictures of us at the party on the internet. She's not too happy about it.' Livid would probably be a better word, but Mel didn't want Jack to know about the tongue-lashing her editor had given her. The general drift of the conversation being that Mel had made the magazine a laughing stock and looked like an unprofessional slut. Then Dansworth had demanded to know why Mel hadn't come up with any juicy exclusives about Jack's past—after all, if you were going to sleep with a guy to get a story, you should at least get the story.

'Damn.' He ran his fingers through his hair, got up and

walked across the study to her. 'Don't look so upset.' He pulled her into his arms, rubbed her back. 'It's none of her business what we do in private.'

She could feel the solid beat of his heart through his sweater. His arms felt so good around her. The smell of him was so familiar and yet so erotic. She wanted so badly to tell him how she felt. But how could she? It would look as if she were begging him to make a commitment. One she now knew he wouldn't want to make. 'She wants me on the next plane home,' she murmured into the soft wool.

'Listen.' He held her away from him, looked into her eyes. 'The article's as good as written, right?'

'Yes.'

'So why don't you email it to her? Then you can tell her where she can shove her job.'

'I…' How she yearned to say yes, but she was forced to think sensibly. 'But I can't do that; I need this job.'

'There are other jobs, and, anyhow, we've still got a date in LA, remember?' He tucked a strand of hair behind her ear, squeezed her shoulder.

'I can't go to LA without a job.' She stepped away from him. 'How will I pay my mortgage when I get home?'

'I can pay your mortgage till you get back on your feet,' he said, frustration clear in his voice.

'I couldn't let you do that.'

'Of course you can—we're sleeping together, honey.'

Mel felt her chest constrict. 'What's that supposed to mean?' The tears she'd been ready to shed shrivelled up inside her. How could he be so flippant about this?

'Hey.' He took her hand, held it. 'Don't get all bent out of shape. All I'm saying is you don't need to be at the mercy of some editor who wouldn't know real literature if Mark Twain came up and socked her on the jaw.'

'Well, actually, I am at her mercy.' She tugged her hand out of his.

He took her arm as she turned away. 'You don't have to go right now, do you? Why don't you take some time to think about it? We can figure out your options.'

She should have said no, she couldn't wait. She should have pointed out that he wasn't giving her any other options. Being his live-in lover was hardly a career choice—and that was all he was offering. In fact, he hadn't even committed to that. A weekend in LA was hardly long-term. But seeing the eagerness in his eyes, and feeling the tingles spread up her arm as his thumb caressed the inside of her elbow, Mel couldn't face the prospect of packing.

'I guess I might as well stay for the rest of the day. I won't be able to get a flight now, anyway.'

Jack let out a breath. 'Great, look, I'm finished here for today. How about we go skating at the Rockefeller Centre? It'll be quiet now and we can grab some supper afterwards, talk about what you're going to do.'

'Go ice-skating?' As an avoidance technique, it had possibilities, Mel realised. She tried to force the worry to the back of her mind. She didn't want to acknowledge how blasé he seemed at the prospect of her leaving. 'I'm not very good at ice-skating.'

'Well, now. That's a shame.' He grinned, gripping her hand and leading her down the hallway. 'I guess I'm just gonna have to keep a real firm hold of you, then.'

Jack kept the dumb grin in place as he bundled Mel into her coat and whisked her out the door.

Hell, Devlin, you nearly blew it, you chump.

Offering to pay for her mortgage had been a mistake. He could have bitten off his tongue the way her back had stiffened as soon as he'd said it. He wouldn't make that mistake again. But no way was he letting her get on any plane and leave him, job or no job.

He droned on about ice-skating and what a beautiful venue the Rockefeller was as he shoved her into a cab. By the time they pulled up outside the impressive venue his jaw was aching from all the cheerful conversation. All of it one-sided. Mel had barely said a word since leaving the apartment.

His plan was a simple one: keep her mind off the whole thing for the next hour or so until he could come up with a convincing argument to get her to stay. He'd panicked back at the apartment when she'd announced she was leaving. He wouldn't do that again. All he had to do was keep calm and keep focused—in a way, the pressure from her editor could turn out to be a good thing. It could force her to come clean with him.

He needed her. He wanted her with him. He'd known it ever since he'd taken her without a condom in the first-class washroom. The prospect of a pregnancy with any other woman would have scared him to death. He'd never wanted to be tied down before, had certainly never considered becoming a father. But as soon as he'd got back to his seat on the plane, he'd realised he didn't feel that way about Mel. The fear of committing himself, the desire to run, simply hadn't come.

On New Year's Eve, with her arms round his neck, her eyes hot on his, he'd figured out something else. She wanted to stay with him. The way she looked at him, the way she made love to him. It wasn't just his ego talking, he was sure of it. He didn't know why she wouldn't admit it, but maybe now things had come to a head she would. He figured it was only pride stopping her.

He watched her as she stared out onto the ice while he ordered their skates from the rental booth. Even when she was bundled up in the wool coat, he could make out her curves. The desire was still as strong and hot as it had ever been. He couldn't seem to get enough of her. It had never been like this before. Usually by now he'd be getting bored, or the woman would be getting ideas that he didn't want to foster. It wasn't like that with Mel. The more he had her, the more he wanted her—right from that first night.

'Here you go, buddy.'

Jack took the heavy boots from the attendant and walked across the concourse to where Mel waited.

As he got closer to her, the blades of the boots cold against his palm, he felt his pulse-rate skid up. Hell, was he falling in love? Sudden panic assailed him and he stopped dead. He forced himself to start walking again. Don't be dumb, Devlin. Of course, he wasn't falling in love. He couldn't be. Hadn't he always promised himself he'd never fall in love? It just made you weak and stupid. He didn't need it, didn't want it. Wasn't even sure he believed in it.

Calm again, and in control, he walked the rest of the way towards her. Resting his hand on her shoulder, he held up her boots when she turned round. 'Here you go, try these on for size.'

She eyed them suspiciously. 'I don't know if this is such a great idea, Jack. The last time I went ice-skating I was about thirteen years old and if I remember rightly I looked a bit like Bambi—legs everywhere!'

He laughed. 'Legs everywhere, huh. Now that's put a very interesting picture in my head.'

Mel could see those tell-tale crinkles as he grinned at her. The teasing light in his eyes. She wanted desperately to share the joke, to dispel the strange ennui that had engulfed her. He was so adorable when he was like this. But the fact he found it so easy to laugh and joke when they had only a few hours left together leeched the usual joy from the situation.

She took the boots, sat down to put them on. His firm, denim-clad thigh pressed against hers on the concrete bench as he pulled on his own boots. Her fingers struggled with the laces.

'Here, let me.' He crouched in front of her and tied the boots. Lifting her chin up with his fist, he forced her eyes to meet his. 'Buck up, Cinders. We'll work something out.'

Mel forced herself to smile.

As she stepped carefully onto the ice his arm tightened around her. She could feel his fingers through the heavy wool of her coat pressing into her waist. She wobbled and he held her steady, tucking her against his side. She could smell the leather of his jacket, feel it warm against her cheek.

'Stop looking at your feet—it'll help,' he said.

She looked up and caught the sudden flash of a thousand tiny lights as the huge three-storey Christmas tree behind the gold fountain at the end of the rink lit up.

'Will you look at that?' he murmured, pressing his lips into her hair. 'Isn't that pretty?'

'Yes,' Mel whispered. What could possibly be more romantic? She squeezed her eyes shut for a moment, willing the tears not to fall. Oh, for Pete's sake, she thought, suddenly sick of being sad. Get over yourself, Rourke. You knew this was bound to happen; you've only got yourself to blame. This is your last evening with the man of your dreams, so stop being silly and make the most of it.

'Come on, let's skate over there,' she said, threading her arm through his. 'But don't you dare let go of me.'

'Not a chance, lady,' he said, kicking off in a smooth glide and taking her—wobbling and clinging on—with him.

They skated for over an hour, until full darkness had fallen and the rink was so packed with people they could barely shuffle round without bumping against another body. It had been hard at first for Mel to forget about what lay ahead, but, as always, being in his arms seemed to push back the doubts, the melancholy. She'd always been a natural optimist, before Adam, and she had to admit, if nothing else, Jack had given that back to her. He was an accomplished skater and before long she gained enough confidence to let him spin her across the ice with him, weaving in and out of the other skaters, enjoying the exhilaration and the intimacy of the chilly New York twilight. And she didn't end up on her bum once, which was a major triumph. Louisa was right: she had some fantastic stories to tell her grandkids.

'Come on, you've had enough,' Jack said as he guided her towards the exit ramp.

'No, I haven't,' Mel replied, determined to savour the moment as long as possible. 'I've got hours in me yet. This is so wonderful.'

'Your nose is blue, you're shivering and you're gonna be sore as hell tomorrow,' Jack said as he grabbed hold of her hand and pulled her out the exit. He plunked her down on the bench and bent down to untie her skates. 'And I don't want you exhausted.' He wiggled his eyebrows wickedly as he eased the boot off. 'I've got plans for tonight that don't involve much sleeping.'

She fisted her hands on her hips and grinned back at him as he took off her other boot. 'And I suppose I don't have any say in that?' she demanded.

'You got that right.' He sat down beside her, unlaced his own boots and pulled them off. 'You've been jiggling around next to me for over an hour.' He stood up, holding his boots, and grabbed hers. Leaning down, he gave her a quick kiss. 'It's time to pay up, Cinders.'

Mel watched him saunter off in his socks towards the skate-hire cubicle. She grinned when he started to whistle, the thrill of anticipation making her even more determined not to think about what was bound to happen tomorrow.

Waiting in line, Jack felt the swell of contentment in his chest. He'd handled that perfectly. He'd take her home now, they could share a lazy bath together, soak off the aches and pains

from all the exercise, before he dealt with another, more insistent ache. Then he'd tell her she was staying with him. He
needed her. And she wanted to stay; he was sure of it. The
simple logic of it seemed so clear. Once he'd got her to admit
it, she wouldn't be able to go.

He was busy imagining her lush breasts covered in soap
suds, the nipples erect, when his eye caught a headline on
the newspaper the guy in front of him in the line was
reading. He squinted, trying to read the copy underneath. It
couldn't be. Could it? He caught his own name, but the print
was too small and the guy was holding it too close for him
to get a proper look. He waited for the line to thin, his agi-
tation building.

As soon as he'd collected Mel's shoes and put on his own,
he stormed over to the nearest news-stand. 'Give me a copy
of *The Post*.'

He scanned through the piece, confusion and anger burning
up the back of his throat as he read it. What the hell was this?
What had she done?

Picking up the shoes that he'd dumped on the floor, he
marched back to her. She sat, her hands tucked between her
legs, staring dreamily at the rink. Her head shot up, though,
when he shoved the paper into her lap.

'Why didn't you tell me you'd been talking to the press?'
he ground out, trying hard not to shout.

Stunned at the accusation in his voice, the rigid expression
on his face, Mel looked down at the newspaper in her lap.
AUTHOR'S LOVER CONFIRMS RUMOURS ABOUT HIS PAST, the
headline screamed back at her.

She picked it up, scanned the contents of the article. 'But,
I never said that; I—'

He whipped the newspaper out of her hands. 'Put your
shoes on. We're going home.'

'Please believe me, Jack,' she began again, humiliated by the pleading in her own voice. 'I didn't say anything about—'

'And I'm telling you,' he cut her off, 'unless you want to fight about this in public, you better put your shoes on.'

Mel had no choice but to swallow her hurt and her humiliation and do as he asked. She could tell by the muscle twitching in his jaw he was about to start shouting.

He refused again to listen to reason as they rode back in the taxi. Only the insistent tap of his foot on the cab floor broke the oppressive silence that settled between them.

By the time the cab braked in front of the apartment building, Mel's rising anger had masked the hurt. How dared he treat her like this, as if she were a child in need of chastisement? She wasn't going to stand for it.

He took her elbow as they walked into the building; she thrust it out of his grasp. 'Don't touch me,' she snapped.

'Don't get all hissy with me,' he growled at her back as she waltzed into the lift. 'I didn't go shooting my mouth off to *The Post*.'

'I told you, I didn't shoot my mouth off to anyone.' She stabbed the button so hard it squeaked. 'If you don't believe me, that's your problem, not mine.'

He grabbed her arm, forced her round to face him as the lift doors swished closed. 'Fine, just explain to me how those quotes got in the paper.'

'No, I won't.' She pulled her arm free again and turned her back on him.

'You owe me an explanation,' he shouted back.

'Too bad you didn't listen earlier, then,' she said with deliberate flippancy, staring at the indicator lights above the lift doors. She could almost hear his teeth grinding together in frustration. Good, let him stew.

The lift bell pinged and she shot out of the doors like a horse under a starter pistol.

'Wait just a minute,' he cried from behind her as she stormed into the apartment. 'How the hell did I get to be the bad guy here?'

The question made her stop, turn back to him. He stood watching her, the confusion plain on his face. Could he really not see it? she wondered.

'What did you think, Jack?' She swallowed to ease the dryness in her throat. 'When you saw that article? Did you think I had gone to *The Post* and told them all your deepest, darkest secrets?'

He looked away, just for a moment, but it was enough to give Mel her answer. Yes, he had. A stab of pain pierced her heart.

'Are you really that cynical, Jack?' she whispered, her voice faltering. How could she have fallen in love with a man who thought so little of her?

She waited for him to say something, anything, but he just shook his head.

'I really think I should go now,' she said, the resignation heavy in her voice and heavier in her heart.

Panic clawed up in Jack's throat as he watched her walk away from him. 'Wait, Mel.' He dashed after her. Fear took over when he got to the bedroom door and watched her place her suitcase calmly on the bed. How had he screwed up so badly?

'I didn't think that, not really. It's just…' He paused, felt the heat rise into his cheeks when she looked at him. 'Okay, I'm kind of paranoid about it.' He tugged frustrated fingers through his hair.

She went to the dresser, opened it. She stared at the contents before turning to look at him. 'Would it really be so terrible if it all came out?'

'Yeah, I think it would.'

'Why, Jack?' She huffed out a breath. 'Your mother was a prostitute. She wasn't a murderer or a child molester. From what you've told me she had a hard life. Maybe you should let go of your anger towards her.'

It wasn't as simple as that, he thought. It couldn't be. 'This isn't about her.'

'Of course it is.' She faced him, the pile of clothes held in her arms like a barrier, annoyance sharpening her voice. 'You don't trust me and that hurts.' She flung the clothes into the suitcase, walked back to the dresser. 'But what's worse is knowing that, no matter what I say or do, you'll probably never trust me.'

He took a step forward, held the drawer shut before she could open it. '*I* don't trust you? That's rich, seeing how you trust me so much.'

'What exactly does that mean?' Mel glared at him, tugging uselessly at the drawer.

'You want to stay with me. Why the hell don't you just admit it? You don't have to go back home and you know it. You're just running scared again.'

Mel let go of the drawer, the demand and the accusation in his words startling her. He was right, she realised. She was running scared. But now she knew why—and her mortgage, her job, had nothing to do with it.

'I *do* have to go.'

'Why?' he said, his voice harsh with annoyance. 'And don't give me all that baloney about your mortgage.'

'I have to go, because I'm in love with you,' she shouted the words back at him.

He let go of the drawer. The stunned expression on his face made her want to weep.

'What?'

'You heard me,' she said, her voice breaking as she pulled the drawer open. Her hands shook as she dumped the last of her clothes into the suitcase and shut the lid.

'Hold on a minute.' He marched over, grabbed the case from her. 'What are you doing?'

'I'm leaving.' She ripped it out of his hands, anger welling up inside her. 'What does it look like?'

'You can't run off now.' He followed her out the bedroom door. 'You just said you loved me.'

'I know, but I'll get over it.' In about a million years, she thought, misery churning in her stomach right alongside the anger.

'So that's all it means to you, is it?' he taunted her. 'You say you love me, but you still pull the old Cinderella routine, right?'

'I'm not the one who's running here, Prince Charming, you are,' she spat back as she flung open the apartment door.

'How do you figure that?' He slapped a hand on the door, slamming it shut.

She glared up at him. 'Do you want to know why I was too scared to tell you, Jack? It wasn't because I didn't trust you; it's because I knew, deep down in my heart, you'd never have the guts to say the words back to me.'

He let his hand fall, wariness plain on his face. 'This isn't about me, it's about you—you're the one who keeps running off every time things get interesting.'

'It's not about me, or you, you idiot. It's about us. I've told you I love you. Yes, I was a coward not to say it sooner. I admit it. But now it's your turn, Jack. I want to know how you feel about me.'

The confusion on his face, the flash of panic in his eyes, made the sting of tears rise back up her throat. He didn't know what to say. This was what she'd been afraid of all along.

'I need more time, to think about it,' he said slowly.

Could he possibly have said anything more humiliating? she thought, forcing the anger back to the surface to cover the pain. 'Well, that's great, Jack. Why don't you take the next twenty years to mull it over? But I'm not going to sit around like a good little woman and wait for you to make up your mind.'

She opened the door, the tearing pain in her heart almost more than she could bear.

'I want you to stay,' he said behind her. 'What more do you want from me?'

She turned back, studied his handsome face rigid with frustration. 'I want you to love me, Jack.' She shook her head. 'And I know you can't.'

She heard him curse loudly as she stepped across the threshold.

The soft sound of the door closing echoed ominously in the cold silence of the entrance lobby. The loud thump from behind it made her flinch as she hurried to the elevator, the tears still lodged painfully in her throat.

Jack kicked the door, hard, the sound of splintering wood satisfying him. She wanted him to grovel and beg—well, she could think again, because he wasn't going to do it.

What did she mean? He couldn't love her. Of course he could, it was just that he didn't want to. Love didn't mean a damn thing. You could say you loved someone, but it didn't mean you really did. You could say you would care for them, look after them, be with them always, but it didn't have to be true. Hadn't his mother taught him that?

Mel was exactly the same. She said all those things but she didn't mean them, not really; she was just saying it to get him to say it too, she wanted him to...

His foot stilled on the door, the picture of Mel hurling the words at him moments before blazing into his mind. He squeezed his eyes shut, shook his head bitterly from side to side. Resting his forehead against the smooth wood, he felt the anger drain out of him. The hollow, empty feeling that replaced it scared him right down to the bone.

She'd been upset and hurt, but she hadn't been lying. She loved him.

What the hell had he done?

Mel walked through the entrance lobby, her head down, her fingers clutched white on the suitcase handle.

'You all right, Mizz Rourke?' the doorman asked as she approached.

She sniffled slightly, quickly wiped the tears from her face. 'I'm fine. Could you get me a cab to the airport, please?'

'Forget the cab, Jerry.' The shouted demand had them both turning to see Jack jogging towards them. As soon as he got to them he pulled the suitcase out of Mel's limp hand and handed it to the doorman. 'Keep that for us, will you, Jerry? We'll be back for it later.'

'Sure thing, Mr Devlin.'

Mel looked from one to the other. 'Excuse me, but that's my suitcase.'

'You won't need it for a while,' Jack said, taking her wrist in his fingers and holding it away from her body. In one fluid movement, he bent forward, shoved his shoulder into her waist and hefted her up in a fireman's lift.

'What are you doing?' she spluttered out, her head banging against his back, still too astonished to struggle. 'Put me down, I'm leaving,' she squealed.

'No, you're not,' he said, conversationally, his hands warm against her thighs as he held her legs in place. 'Not this time.'

She wiggled then, pushed her hands against his back, tried to arch up. 'For goodness' sake, put me down. This is embarrassing.'

'Tough.'

She could see Jerry the doorman smiling at them both as she bounced back towards the lift. Heat flooded into her cheeks. 'Jack, I mean it. Leave us some dignity.'

'The hell with dignity,' was all he said.

The lift doors slid open instantly. She tried to grab hold of the frame as he waltzed through, but missed.

This was ridiculous. She was practically in tears and he was behaving like a madman. She made a fist and thumped him hard on the back.

He grunted and dropped her, but before she could scramble away he grabbed her hips and trapped her against the lift wall, flattening his body against hers. The carpeted panelling felt rough against the thin silk of her blouse as his chest flattened her breasts and his thighs pressed hard against hers. She felt the instant response, the prickling heat at her nipples, the pulsing fire at her core, and her cheeks blazed. She tried to bring her hands up to push him away, but he clamped his hands round her wrists and held them down.

'Stop it, Jack.' She wriggled; his big body didn't budge an inch. 'It isn't funny.'

'You don't hear me laughing, do you?' he said in a strained voice. He turned slightly and she realised he was as affected as she was, the bulge in his jeans all too obvious.

She stilled, frantically trying to think of another tactic.

She would not break down in front of him, no matter what. If that was what he hoped to achieve from this little charade, she was not going to oblige. He'd played her all the way along, seducing her, romancing her, making her fall in love with him. For what? All so that he could tell her he didn't love her in return. She didn't have a great deal of pride left, but the little she had she was going to cling onto like a cliff edge.

'We're not having farewell sex, if that's what this is about,' she said, struggling to keep her voice even.

He gave a mirthless laugh. 'Forget about that. I can't help it. It'll go down in a minute if you stop wriggling.'

'I want you to let me go,' she said with as much dignity as she could muster while feeling his still-prominent erection prodding her. Even with the several layers of clothes between them she could feel it pulsing; she was sure of it.

The lift doors slid open at the penthouse again and he stepped back suddenly. She couldn't help her eyes flitting down to his groin. They shot straight back up again.

'What do you want?' she said.

He gave her a wry smile, but his eyes were dark and serious. 'Apart from the obvious, you mean?'

'Yes.'

'I want to talk, that's all.'

'I think we've said enough.' She didn't think she could bear any more, she realised. Her insides felt so raw, so vulnerable already.

'Will you at least come in and listen to what I've got to say?'

'Jack.' She sighed, not sure if she could hold out against the tenderness in his eyes, knowing she must. 'What's the point?'

'Ten minutes, that's all I'm asking for.' He took her hand in his, stroked her fingers. The familiar caress made her heart squeeze. 'After that I'll call you a cab myself,' he continued. 'I want a chance to set things right.'

So that was what this was all about, she thought, miserably. He wanted to make amends, to part without bad feelings. She thought about what Alicia had said about how he'd tried to let her friend Catherine down easily. It was important to him; she could see that by the intensity in his face.

'Okay,' she said wearily.

He led her back into the apartment, putting a hand gently on the small of her back as he had so many times before. She walked into the living area, perched carefully on one of the armchairs, determined not to break, no matter what.

'Do you want a drink?' he said.

'No.' How long was he going to drag this out?

'Do you mind if I get one?'

She shook her head, made even more tense by his politeness.

His erection had subsided, she noticed with relief when he turned towards her with a shot glass of whiskey in his hand. He slugged it down in one go. Why didn't he just say it, so she could go and start trying to rebuild her life?

She waited, but still he didn't speak. Instead, he walked to the wall of windows, stood there, his feet braced apart, looking down at the darkness of Central Park for what seemed like an eternity. Why was his back so rigid? Why wouldn't he look at her?

'You were right,' he said at last.

'About what?'

'I couldn't say it.'

'Say what?'

He turned, stared at her. 'I couldn't say I love you.'

The tear spilled over before she could stop it. She stood up, brushed it away with a trembling hand. 'You brought me back to tell me you don't love me, again?' she demanded, incredulously. Why was he doing this? Did he want to see her break?

He bolted across the room, gripped her arms before she could get away.

'No, no, you don't understand. That's not what I meant.'

'What did you mean?' she said, her whole body shaking with pain and regret, the tears flowing freely now.

'I couldn't say it because until you came along, they were just empty words to me.'

He let go of her, sat down. Propping his elbows onto his knees, he sank his head into his hands. 'I said them to her and she left me anyway.'

She still wasn't sure what he was trying to say, but, seeing his vulnerability, knowing how hard it was for him to talk about, she did the only thing she could do. She sat beside him, laid a comforting hand on his back. 'Will you tell me about it?'

'There's not much to tell.' His voice was muffled. 'I thought I'd handled it, but I'm still angry with her.' He turned to look at her. 'You were right about that too.' He buried his head back in his hands. 'Why didn't she get clean? Why didn't she look after me properly? Why did she leave me with him?' He sighed.

She kept stroking his back, the sorrow inside her for the child he'd been overwhelming her. 'You missed her,' she said simply.

'Yeah.' He nodded, lifting his head. 'Yeah, I guess I did. But I did something really dumb. I let what happened with her rule my life. You said that too, didn't you?'

She nodded, the knowledge bitter-sweet. Maybe now he understood that about himself, he would be able to love someone, some day, even if it couldn't be her.

He shifted on the seat, took her hands in his and pressed his forehead against hers. 'I'm through doing that now. So.' He drew a long, careful breath, pulled back; his eyes met hers. 'You asked me how I feel about you and I lied.'

'I don't understand.' She felt the fluttering in her stomach at the intensity in his voice.

'I said I had to think about it, which was, well, garbage, really.'

'Oh.'

'Yeah, oh.' She heard him swallow, saw his jaw tense. 'Ever since we made love that first time, I haven't been able to stop wanting you. And, believe me, I've tried.' His fingers tightened on her hands. 'I get a real kick out of it when I can make you laugh, and it hurts, a lot, when I make you cry. I've never needed anyone before in my life, never wanted anyone with me, but I want you.' He looked up, a guilty expression in his eyes. 'And, I'll tell you something else. I wouldn't mind a bit if you were pregnant right now. In fact, I'd be kind of overjoyed.' He let go of her hands, cupped her cheeks in his palms. 'Now, I don't know if that's love, but I think it might be. I could say the words to you, but I'd rather show you. If you'll let me.'

Mel's heart was beating so hard, so fast, she was sure it would burst. 'You're pretty good with words.' She smiled, her body floating on a wave of excitement and euphoria. 'When you want to be.'

'You bet,' he said. His hands dropped from her face. 'But that's not an answer.'

She lifted her hands, threaded her fingers through his thick black hair. Pulling him close, she flicked her tongue across his bottom lip. 'The question is, Mr Devlin…' she nibbled kisses across his jaw, heard his sharp intake of breath '…do you want me to tell you or show you?'

He gripped her waist, tried to pull her tight against him, making their knees bump together. He stood up, hauled her off the couch and swung her into his arms. She slung her hands round his neck, laughing, as she leaned in for another kiss.

'But that's not an answer either.' She giggled, revelling in the giddy rush of love and arousal as she kissed the rough bristles along his jaw.

'Give me a minute. I'm getting to it,' he said in a frustrated voice as he strode into the bedroom, her laughter trailing behind them.

EPILOGUE

THE butterflies in Mel's belly were re-enacting the Battle of Britain as she stared out of the bookstore's window at the queue of people winding down Piccadilly in the rain.

'Mel, there you are.' Louisa walked to her side through the darkened office. 'What are you doing hiding up here? Everything's ready downstairs.'

Mel turned to her friend. 'I can't believe so many people came,' she said, dazed.

'You've got to be joking,' Louisa replied, her lips curving. 'The reviews were fantastic, you've been at the top of Amazon's advance sales list for months and then there's the whirlwind romance between you and the subject to add to the publicity-coup factor.' Louisa sighed. 'For goodness' sake, Mel. The release of *Devlin: The Man Behind the Mystery* has to be the most eagerly awaited event in the publishing calendar for about a decade. It's no surprise people turned up in their droves.'

Mel looked back out of the window. 'I'm so nervous my hands are shaking.'

Louisa put her arm round Mel's waist and gave her a quick hug. 'Don't be silly, Mel. What have you got to be nervous about? You've already done the hard part. You've married the man of your dreams, given him a beautiful baby daughter and written what's likely to be one of the biggest-selling biographies in the history of biographies. And all in the space of two years.'

Mel felt the swell of happiness in her chest at Louisa's words. The nerves retreated a little. 'I suppose you've got a point.'

'Of course I've got a point. It's another one of those no-brainers, you ninny.'

Mel smiled, remembering the day when Louisa had used the term once before. The two years since had been an incredible roller-coaster ride of love, passion and life-altering challenges and she wouldn't have missed a second of them for all the panic attacks in the world.

'Now.' Louisa grasped her hand and led her towards the office door. 'All you've got to do is sign a few thousand books, make nice to an assortment of the buying public and smile for the cameras for two hours solid. It'll be a cinch.'

'Well, of course, when you put it like that…' Mel's words trailed off as she followed Louisa through the door.

'Where is the Mystery Man, anyway? I thought he'd be here?'

The mention of her husband made Mel's confidence lift another crucial notch. 'He's coming later.'

Although she'd left him less than an hour ago, Mel was already anticipating his arrival. Would the love she felt for him never lose its intensity? She certainly hoped not.

'He didn't want to steal my thunder,' she continued. 'And he had to settle Ella for the night at Christy and Meg's. You know what she's like—she won't go to sleep unless her daddy reads her a bedtime story.'

'Yes, and we all know what a chore her daddy finds that.' Louisa smiled as she pushed open the door to the stairwell. 'How is the queen of the universe anyway? I haven't seen her for nearly two weeks.'

Mel laughed at the accuracy of Louisa's description. At fifteen months, with her corkscrew black curls and her bright, fiendishly intelligent blue eyes, Ella Valentine Devlin was the ruler of all she surveyed—and, boy, did she know it.

Mel could still remember the shock when she'd discovered her initiation into the mile-high club had resulted in a pregnancy. Without a job and still in the first flush of love, Mel had panicked, convinced that a child so soon would be a disaster. She and Jack had been going out for less than a month. They hadn't even decided where they were going to live. How could they possibly cope with the responsibility of a baby?

To her astonishment, Jack had refused to talk about any of her concerns. He had been ecstatic about the baby. He'd wanted her to have it. Whether she did or not had boiled down to one simple question in his mind. Did she want to have it too? Once he'd got his answer, the discussion had been over.

Jack had bought a house in Regent's Park and demanded they get married. Then, when Mel had been two months pregnant, coping with the horrors of morning sickness and struggling to make a career out of her book reviews and the articles she'd begun writing for a string of literary magazines, Jack had suggested she write his biography.

Once again, she'd panicked. Would she be good enough? She didn't have any experience as a biographer. Wouldn't it look unprofessional if his wife wrote his biography? What about the misery of Jack's childhood? Did he really want it put into print?

And once again Jack's response had been pithy and to the point. He trusted her. He wanted her to write it. Did she want to do it or not?

Working on the book had become an incredible journey for them both. During her research, they had returned to the tiny mid-western town where Jack had grown up. After much nagging from her, Jack had agreed to attend a special dinner in his honour arranged by the city council. Seeing him fêted by the people who had once rejected him had brought tears to Mel's eyes. As the speeches had been given, an award made,

Mel had whispered to him how proud she was of him. He had brushed the compliment aside, insisting her sentimental reaction was due to the pregnancy hormones. But when they had made love that night in the town's only motel, he had been so tender, so careful with her, she had known how much the evening had meant to him. He'd laid the ghosts of his past to rest at last.

Two months later, three scant days after the finished manuscript had been emailed to the publishers, their daughter had put in her appearance. Ella had turned out to be a bigger challenge than either of them could possibly have guessed. But the little minx had wrapped her chubby little fingers round their hearts from the first moment they'd met her.

'She's added a new word to her vocabulary.' Mel smiled, thinking of her daughter's newest accomplishment as she and Louisa walked down the service corridor towards the bookstore's shop floor. 'And she's really pleased with it. I think it's going to get a lot of use from now on.'

'Surely it's not going to supersede the ever-popular "Daddy" and "No"?' Louisa said, her heels clicking rhythmically on the concrete.

'The new word's "mine" and, believe me, Christy's girls Sofia and Isabel didn't know what had hit them when she got to their house this afternoon and started claiming all their toys. Poor old Jack, I had to leave him to handle it,' Mel said, not feeling nearly as contrite as she should have.

'I wish I'd been there.' Louisa laughed. 'I'd love to have seen Mr Super-Cool trying to referee a toddlers' catfight.'

'I don't think it's one of his fortes.' Mel grinned, remembering how cute he'd looked doing it.

'Right, we're here.' Louisa stopped in front of the large double doors leading to the shop floor.

Through the glass panels, Mel could see the signing table laden with several tidy piles of her books, the small group of publishing, press and PR people and the line of eager customers clutching copies to sign. Her pulse rate bumped back up and the butterflies kicked off another dogfight in her stomach.

'You ready?' Louisa said, concern in her voice.

Mel's eyes settled on the billboard of her book cover behind the signing table. Jack's handsome face stared back at her, his expression enigmatic, his gaze penetrating. A flash of remembrance came to her, the first time she'd looked into that intense, vivid blue two years before in this very bookshop. The same sharp thrill of arousal came to her, but it was deeper and so much more potent now she knew the promise of what lay behind it. She turned to Louisa and gave her a shaky smile. 'Yes, I think I am.' Passing her friend, she pushed open the door and walked into the mêlée, nerves and excitement doing a tug of war inside her.

Two hours later, Mel's fingers were cramping, her bum ached from sitting down for so long and she felt frazzled. Where on earth was Jack? She needed him.

As she registered the thought a hush came over the crowd and the elderly lady whose book she'd just signed murmured, 'Goodness, I think my heart just stopped.'

Mel turned to see her husband standing a few feet away, deep in conversation with the publisher's PR man. He was in faded jeans, a simple polo-neck jumper and his favourite battered leather jacket, his long, wavy hair combed back from his forehead in sexy disarray, and Mel knew exactly what the old lady meant.

Mel studied him as he put a hand on the PR guy's shoulder and then turned. His eyes fixed on her and her heart jolted in her chest. The line of people leading back from the table fell silent as he walked over to her, leaned down and, cupping her cheek in his palm, kissed her full on the lips. Mel was sure her skin had flushed scarlet by the time he lifted his head. The spontaneous round of applause from their audience didn't help a bit.

'How you doing, Cinders?' he whispered.

'I think I'm on fire.'

'Good, hold that thought.' He grinned, the sexual promise clear in his eyes. 'I spoke to the PR guy and he's going to cap the line. I should be able to spring you in no time.'

No time turned out to be nearly an hour later once the last of the customers had been sent off with their signed copies and the bookstore staff properly thanked for all their hard work.

'Now I know why you whine so much about book signings.' Mel sighed, enjoying the warm weight of Jack's arm around her shoulders as they left the shop. 'That was exhausting.'

'Hey, I don't whine.' Jack pulled back, gave her an affronted look. 'I take my punishment like a man.'

Mel smiled up at him. 'Which would explain why you moaned for three days about your sore wrist after your last signing.'

'Okay, fine,' he said, resting his arm on her waist and guiding her through the Saturday shoppers racing to get their purchases home. 'Don't expect sympathy when your fingers stiffen up tomorrow.'

'Actually, it's not my fingers that are hurting.'

He stopped and looked down at her, the teasing light gone from his eyes. 'Where are you hurting?' he asked.

'It's my bum,' she said, loving the way his eyes darkened at the mention of that particular part of her anatomy. 'I think I may have saddle sores after sitting in that chair for so long.'

'Yeah?' The blue of his irises deepened still further as he pushed his hands under her coat, rested them on her backside. 'You know what?' he said, his voice low as he pulled her against him, his fingers massaging her through the wool of her dress. 'I've got the perfect cure for that particular problem.'

The delicious heat rising from her core made Mel moan, before she remembered where they were. 'Perhaps we should get a cab, doctor, before you start treating me in the street.'

He chuckled, gave her rump a quick pat, and released her. 'No need,' he said, gripping her hand. 'I've got something better planned.'

It was only then that she realised they'd stopped outside the entrance to The Ritz. He'd pulled her past the liveried doorman and into the lavish marble entrance lobby before she got her voice back. 'What are we doing here?' she said.

He raised one dark brow and grinned at her. 'You owe me, Cinders. I figure it's high time you paid up.'

With that audacious statement he turned to the hotel clerk and checked them into the Royal Suite.

Mel's pulse skidded into overdrive as they walked into the suite. The deluxe gold and leather décor was exactly as she remembered it. A bottle of champagne sat in an ice bucket on the table where they'd once flirted over steak and potatoes. Mel felt herself flush at the thought of the wild, wonderful night of passion that had changed her life.

Jack slipped off her coat, turned her to face him. 'I love the way you still do that,' he murmured, his thumb cool as it skimmed over the heat in her cheek. He held her chin and placed a light kiss on her lips.

'So what is it that I owe you, Prince Charming?' she whispered against his mouth, her fingers caressing the hair at his nape. Her heart pounded with longing as she felt him shudder in response.

'Well, now.' His hands trailed up her back. She felt the smooth ripple as he tugged the zip of her dress down. 'It has to do with this real vivid sexual fantasy that's been bugging me ever since that night.'

'Oh, really?' She choked the words out as he pulled the dress off and unsnapped her bra.

'I figured we'd get to it first thing in the morning, but when I woke up, you'd split.' The heat throbbed viciously at her core as he stroked her naked breasts.

'And what exactly did this sexual fantasy of yours entail?' she said, her voice breaking on a shaky sigh as his thumbs circled her nipples.

'Let's get you into the shower and I'll show you,' he said, nipping her bottom lip.

She laughed as he lifted her into his arms, every nerve ending tingling with arousal and anticipation.

'And remember, Cinders,' he said, his voice forbidding as he marched through the dimly lit bedroom and pushed open the bathroom door with his butt, 'there's gonna be no running out on me tomorrow morning—or there'll be serious consequences.'

Mel kissed the rough skin of his jaw, knowing she would never run from him again—no matter what the consequences.